REBECCA

REBECCA

Published 2024 by Maple Spring Publishing

Front cover design by David Rheinhardt of Pyrographx
Interior design by Jason Snyder.

Library of Congress Cataloging-in-Publication Data is available upon request

ISBN: 979-8-3505-0096-7

10 9 8 7 6 5 4 3 2 1

REBECCA

Directed by Alfred Hitchcock

Produced by David O. Selznick

Screenplay by Robert E. Sherwood *and* Joan Harrison

Based on the novel by Daphne du Maurier

Adapted by Philip MacDonald *and* Michael Hogan

Music by Franz Waxman

Art direction by Lyle Wheeler

Photography by George Barnes

Special effects by Jack Gosbrove

Film editor: Hal C. Kern

CAST

MAXIM de Winter . . . . Lawrence Olivier

Mrs. de Winter . . . . Joan Fontaine

Jack Flavell . . . . George Sanders

Mrs. Danvers . . . . Judith Anderson

Giles . . . . Nigel Bruce

Frank Crawley . . . . Reginald Denny

Colonel Julyan . . . . C. Aubrey Smith

Beatrice . . . . Gladys Cooper

Mrs. Van Hopper. . . . . Florence Bates

The Coroner . . . . Melville Cooper

Dr. Baker. . . . . Leo C. Carroll

Ben . . . . Leonard Carey

Tabb . . . . Lumsden Hare

Frith . . . . Edward Fielding

Robert. . . . . Philip Winter

Charlcroft. . . . . Forrester Harvey

eneath the blackened stonework is a once fine old English house of early Tudor style. Above the window frames, gaping holes tell us that the building is nothing but a burnt-out shell. The once magnificent gardens are an overgrown mass of weeds. At the end of the driveway, the growth is jungle-like.

"I's" VOICE

Last night I dreamt I went to Manderley again. It seemed to me I stood by the iron gate leading to the drive, and for a while I could not enter, for the way was barred to me. Then, like all dreamers, I was possessed of a sudden with supernatural powers and passed like a spirit through the barrier before me. The drive wound away in front of me, twisting and turning as it had always done. But as I advanced, I was aware that a change had come upon it. Nature had come into her own again and little by little had encroached upon the drive with long tenacious fingers. On and on wound the poor thread that had once been our drive. And finally there was Manderley. Manderley, secretive and silent. Time could not mar the perfect symmetry of those walls. Moonlight can play odd tricks upon the fancy and suddenly it seemed to me that light came from the windows. And then a cloud came upon the moon and hovered an instant like a dark hand before a face. The illusion went with it. I looked upon a desolate shell with no whisper of the past about its staring walls. We can never go back to Manderley again, that much is certain. But sometimes, in my dreams, I do go back to the strange days of my life which began for me in the south of France.

Manderley was the most beautiful house I ever saw—a thing of grace, exquisite and faultless. Its clean grey stone had been mellowed by the centuries. Time could not harm the perfect symmetry of these walls. Its shining mullioned windows looked down upon bright gardens and trim velvet lawns which swept in terrace after terrace to the sea . . . We can never go back there again. The past is still too close to us. But sometimes in my dreams I do go back . . .

(pause)

. . . to the strange days of my life which began, for me, on the top of a cliff, in the South of France . . .

In the South of France, MAXIM, with an agonized look on his face, is standing upon a precipice, watching the angry sea dashing itself against some rocks.

He is almost about to take a fatal step. Suddenly there is a tiny scream behind him.

"I"

No! Stop!

MAXIM's head turns quickly, and, as though just passing, is a young girl of twenty: "I." He commences to stride towards her.

SEMI CLOSE UP

MAXIM

Who are you? What the devil are you staring at?

"I"

I'm sorry, I didn't mean to stare. Only I thought . . .

MAXIM

Oh, you're English, are you! What are you doing here?

• 2 •

"I"

I was only walking . . . I . . .

MAXIM

Well, get on with your walking—don't hang about here screaming.

The girl hastens away.

LONG SHOT—INT.—EARLY EVENING

In the lounge of the Hotel de Paris, it is evening. MRS. VAN HOPPER, an upper-class middle-aged English snob, is surveying the assemblage through her lorgnette and indicating acute distaste. "I" is sitting next to her.

MRS. VAN HOPPER

I'll never come to Monte Carlo out of season again. There isn't a single well-known personality in the hotel.

MRS. VAN HOPPER sips her coffee, and makes a face.

MRS. VAN HOPPER

Stone cold!

As a WAITER passes by, she calls after him.

MRS. VAN HOPPER

Waiter. Garçon. Call him. Tell him to get me some—

MRS. VAN HOPPER's expression changes as she looks across the lounge and sees MAXIM DE WINTER, the man who was at the top of the cliff. MRS. VAN HOPPER'S expression shows that she is preparing to greet an old friend gushingly.

MRS. VAN HOPPER

Why! It's Max de Winter.

As MAXIM comes nearer to them, we see that "I" is awed by his approach. She starts to rise from her armchair, her hands gripping the arms. But MAXIM looks straight through "I" as though he had never seen her before and steers himself through the furniture to pass them. MRS. VAN HOPPER smiles eagerly and inclines her head.

MRS. VAN HOPPER

Mr. de Winter! How do you *do*?!

MAXIM looks at her. He is not sure where or when he met her, or what her name is. He is only sure that he doesn't want to see her now.

MAXIM *(uncertainly)*

How do you do.

MRS. VAN HOPPER

I'm Edith Van Hopper. It's *so* nice to run into you here, just when I was beginning to *despair* of finding any old friends in Monte . . . But do sit down and have some coffee.

MRS. VAN HOPPER turns to "I."

Mr. de Winter is having coffee with me. Go and ask that stupid waiter for another cup.

MAXIM

I'm afraid I must contradict you. You are both having coffee with me. Garçon!

MRS. VAN HOPPER

You know, I recognized you just as soon as you walked into the restaurant. Even though I haven't seen you since that night at the Casino in Palm Beach.

(provocatively)

But perhaps you don't remember an old woman like me . . . Are you playing the tables much here at Monte?

MAXIM

No. I'm afraid that sort of thing ceased to amuse me years ago.

MRS. VAN HOPPER

I can well understand it. As for me, if I had a home like Manderley, I'd certainly never come to Monte. I hear it's one of the biggest places in that part of the country and that you just can't beat it for beauty.

MAXIM does not answer, but turns to "I."

MAXIM

And what do you think of Monte Carlo? Or don't you think of it at all?

"I" *(embarrassed and tremblingly)*
I—I'm afraid I find it rather artificial . . . I . . .

MRS. VAN HOPPER *(annoyed, interrupting)*
She's spoilt, Mr. de Winter. That's her trouble. Most girls would give their eyes for the chance to see Monte.

MAXIM

Wouldn't that rather defeat the purpose?

MRS. VAN HOPPER *(impervious to the dig)*

Now that we've found each other again, I hope I shall see something of you. You must come and have a drink in my suite . . . I hope they've given you a good room? The place is empty, so if you're uncomfortable, mind you make a fuss. Your valet has unpacked for you, I suppose?

MAXIM

I'm afraid I don't possess one. Perhaps you'd like to do it for me?

MRS. VAN HOPPER *(at last embarrassed)*

Well—I hardly think—

MRS. VAN HOPPER turns to "I."

MRS. VAN HOPPER

Perhaps you can make yourself useful to Mr. de Winter if he wants anything done. You're a capable child in many ways.

MAXIM *(with a faint sardonic smile)*

That's a charming suggestion. But I'm afraid I cling to the old motto: "He travels fastest who travels alone." Perhaps you've not heard of it.

MAXIM rises, bows, and exits.

MRS. VAN HOPPER

What do you make of that! Do you suppose that sudden departure was intended to be funny?

MRS. VAN HOPPER says to "I":

Come. Don't sit there gawking. Have you got the key? Let's go upstairs.

"I" and MRS. VAN HOPPER cross the lobby toward the elevator.

MRS. VAN HOPPER (*without stopping*)
I remember when I was younger, there was a well-known writer who used to dart down the back way whenever he saw me coming. I suppose he was in love with me and wasn't sure of himself . . . Well, c'est la vie!

MRS. VAN HOPPER turns to "I."

By the way, my dear, don't think I mean to be unkind, but you were just a teeny-weeny bit forward with Mr. de Winter. Your effort to enter the conversation quite embarrassed me, as I'm sure it did him. Men loathe that sort of thing.

"I" shrivels at this attack.

MRS. VAN HOPPER
Oh come, don't sulk. After all, I am responsible for your behavior here.

They are now nearly at the elevator.

MRS. VAN HOPPER
Perhaps he didn't notice it.

As they enter the elevator, MRS. VAN HOPPER says,

Poor thing, I suppose he just can't get over his wife's death.

As "I" turns around from entering the lift, she looks at MRS. VAN HOPPER but doesn't answer.

MRS. VAN HOPPER
They say he simply adored her.

The next day at lunchtime, "I," carrying a portfolio of her sketching paraphernalia, comes into the dining room. The HEADWAITER comes forward. He turns her over to a subordinate to take her to her table across the enormous, almost empty room. Two or three tables away is MAXIM, alone. She is embarrassed and self-conscious as she walks toward her table.

In unfolding her napkin, she awkwardly knocks over a small vase of flowers. The waiter comes in quickly to take away the vase and the sprawling flowers.

"I" *(to waiter)*
How awkward! Please don't bother. It doesn't matter.

MAXIM comes up to them.

MAXIM *(to waiter)*
Leave that—and set another place at my table. Mademoiselle will have lunch with me.

"I"
Oh, no—I couldn't possibly.

MAXIM
Why not?

"I"
Please don't be polite. It's very kind of you, but I shall be all right if the waiter just changes the cloth.

MAXIM
But I'm not being polite. I'd have asked you to have luncheon with me even if you hadn't knocked over that vase so clumsily. We needn't talk to each other unless we feel like it.

"I"

Thank you very much.

She rises, and they seat themselves at MAXIM'S table. MAXIM'S luncheon is already on the table. The headwaiter comes to the table and hands a menu to "I."

"I" *(to the waiter)*

I'll just have some scrambled eggs, please.

WAITER

Oui, Mademoiselle.

The WAITER exits with the menu.

MAXIM

What's happened to your friend?

"I"

She's ill in bed with a cold.

MAXIM

I'm sorry I was so rude to you yesterday. The only excuse I can make is that I've become boorish through living alone . . .

"I"

Oh, you weren't, really. You simply wanted to be alone, and—

MAXIM

Tell me: is Mrs. Van Hopper a friend of yours? Or just a relation?

"I"

No, she's my employer. I'm what is known as a paid companion.

MAXIM

I didn't know that companionship could be bought.

"I" *(with a smile)*

I once looked up the word "companion" in the dictionary. It said "a friend of the bosom."

MAXIM

I don't envy you the privilege.

"I"

She's very kind, really, and—and—I have to earn my living.

MAXIM

Haven't you any family?

"I"

No, my mother died years and years ago, and then there was only my father. He died last summer. And then I took this job.

MAXIM

How rotten for you.

"I"

Yes, it was, you see, because we got on so well together.

MAXIM

You and your father?

"I"

Yes—a lovely person. Very unusual.

MAXIM

What was he?

"I"

A painter.

MAXIM

Ah, was he a good one?

"I"

Well, I thought so. But people didn't understand.

MAXIM

Well, that's often the trouble.

"I"

He painted trees. At least it was one tree.

MAXIM

You mean he painted the same tree over and over again?

"I"

Yes, you see, he had a theory that if you should find one perfect thing or place or person, you should stick to it. Do you think that's very silly?

MAXIM

No, not at all. I feel very much like that myself. And what did you find to do with yourself while he was painting his tree?

"I"

I sat for him, and I sketched a little. I don't do it very well, though.

MAXIM sees "I"'s sketching portfolio.

Oh, you're going sketching this afternoon? Where?

"I" *(embarrassed)*

Well. I hadn't made up my mind.

MAXIM

I'll drive you somewhere in the car.

"I"

Oh, but really, I didn't mean to . . .

MAXIM *(interrupting)*

Nonsense. Finish up that mess and we'll get along.

During this, "I" has not touched her eggs at all.

"I"

Oh, thank you . . . It's very kind of you . . . but I'm not very hungry.

MAXIM

Come on—eat it up like a good girl.

"I" shyly, rather embarrassed, lifts a forkful of egg to her mouth, keeping her eyes on MAXIM.

On a terrace balcony overlooking Monte Carlo is a long flight of steps, with a terrace, leading down to the sea. At the top of the stairs is MAXIM's car.

"I" is seated on the terrace, apparently sketching the view. MAXIM leans over the railing of the balcony, gazing at the bay. Then he glances over towards "I."

MAXIM

You're taking a long time with that sketch. I shall expect a really fine work of art.

"I" begins feverishly to rub out, as she protests:

"I"

Oh, no, don't look at it. . . it's not nearly good enough.

MAXIM *(getting to his feet)*

It can't be as bad as all that. Let me see before it's all rubbed out.

As MAXIM comes over and stands behind her, "I" tries to cover up her sketch with her hands to prevent him seeing it.

"I"

It's the perspective. I never *can* get it right.

MAXIM's expression as he looks at the sketch changes to one of comic surprise. It is a badly done, childish drawing of himself.

MAXIM *(interrupting with mock gravity)*

Do you think it's the perspective that makes my nose take such a bend in the middle?

Seeing that he is only amused and in no way offended, "I" takes her cue from his mood, and smiles back happily at him, as she answers in her own defense.

"I"

You're not a very easy subject—your expression keeps changing all the time.

 (pointing out to sea)
Does it? I'd concentrate on the view instead, if I were you—much more worthwhile. Rather reminds me of our coastline at home.

"I" follows him, and they sit facing each other on the railing.

MAXIM *(suddenly)*
Do you know Cornwall at all?

"I"
Yes, I was there once with my father on holiday. I was in a shop once, and I saw a postcard with a beautiful house on it right by the sea. I asked what house it was, and the old woman said, "That's Manderley." I felt ashamed for not knowing.

MAXIM
Manderley is beautiful. To me, it's just the place where I was born, I've lived in all my life. Now I don't suppose I shall ever see it again.

MAXIM doesn't answer. He is lost in thought, looking out to sea. There is a silence while "I" thinks of something to say. She looks around for inspiration down toward the shore. Then turning back to her companion, with a great effort she starts to chat.

"I"
We're lucky to be away from home during the bad weather, aren't we? I can't ever remember being able to enjoy swimming in England till about June, can you?

MAXIM fails to react to her efforts. He remains silent.

"I"

The water's so warm here—I could stay in all day. Though there's a dangerous undertow—a man was drowned here last year . . . I've never had any fear of drowning, have you?

There is still no response from her companion. She turns to look at him. MAXIM is no longer seated beside her. He is standing at the other end of the stone balcony, motionless, staring out to sea. After a moment he swings round and comes forward with a grim expression. "I" is still looking at MAXIM unhappily, unable to understand what she has said to upset him. She gives a little shiver, half of apprehension, half of cold.

MAXIM

Come, I'll take you home.

Back in the hotel, "I" hurries up to the door of MRS. VAN HOPPER's suite. She pauses a moment outside, then goes in. MRS. VAN HOPPER is propped up in bed. Standing beside the bed, a nurse is measuring out some medicine.

MRS. VAN HOPPER

Oh, yes, I knew Mr. de Winter well. I knew his wife too. Before she married she was the beautiful Rebecca Hildreth, you know. She was drowned, poor dear . . . while she was sailing . . . near Manderley. He never talks about it, of course, but he's a broken man.

The NURSE gives MRS. VAN HOPPER some medicine, which she swallows.

MRS. VAN HOPPER

Wretched stuff! Give me a chocolate, quick!

To "I," MRS. VAN HOPPER says,

MRS. VAN HOPPER

Oh, *there* you are. And it's about time. Hurry up, I want to play some rummy.

FADE OUT.

FADE IN:
INT. "I'S" BEDROOM—
CLOSE SHOT—NIGHT

"I" is asleep in bed. The moonlight streams across her. Her head shirts with a faint movement now and again. As she tosses and turns, we hear MRS. VAN HOPPER'S VOICE.

MRS. VAN HOPPER

She was the beautiful Rebecca Hildreth, you know. . . They say he simply adored her . . . She was the beautiful Rebecca Hildreth, you know. . . I suppose he just can't get over his wife's death. She was the beautiful Rebecca Hildreth, you know . . . but he's a broken man . . .

FADE IN:
INT. MRS. VAN HOPPER'S SUITE—
SEMI CLOSE UP—DAY

MRS. VAN HOPPER is still propped up in bed. "I" comes in, brightly, with a tennis racket.

MRS. VAN HOPPER

Well, where are you going?

"I"

I thought I'd take a tennis lesson.

MRS. VAN HOPPER

I see. I suppose you had a look at the pro, and he's desperately handsome, and you've conceived a school-girl crush on him? All right, go ahead, make the most of it!

As "I" walks through the lobby toward the main door, she stops short at the sound of MAXIM's voice.

MAXIM

Off duty?

"I"

Yes, Mrs. Van Hopper's cold has turned to flu, so she's got a trained nurse.

MAXIM

I'm sorry for the nurse . . . Are you keen on tennis?

"I"

Not particularly, but—

MAXIM *(taking the racket from her)*

Good! We'll go for a drive.

MAXIM puts the racket behind a potted palm and, taking her arm, leads her towards the revolving door.

We see MAXIM and "I," driving contentedly but in silence along a country road.

DISSOLVE TO:
INT. MRS. VAN HOPPER'S ROOM—
SEMI CLOSE UP—DAY

Back in the hotel, "I" enters MRS. VAN HILDRETH's room, with her tennis racket, beaming. MRS. VAN HOPPER is still in bed.

MRS. VAN HOPPER

You've been gone for *hours*! You got on rather well with him, didn't you?

"I" is startled by this question. She doesn't know how to reply.

MRS. VAN HOPPER

That pro must have been teaching you other things than tennis . . . Now hurry up. I want you to make some calls.

MRS. VAN HOPPER puts out her cigarette in a jar of cleansing cream.

MRS. VAN HOPPER

I wonder if Mr. de Winter is still in the hotel.

We see a close-up of a handwritten letter:

> *"Dear Mr. de Winter: Why don't you return my calls, you naughty man!*
> *"As soon as I get over this nasty old cold, I promise to keep you from being bored here in Monte. Because I know that's just what you must be—bored, bored, bored!*
> *"In fond friendship, Edythe Van Hopper"*

The scene then turns to a formal outdoor dance on the patio, both "I" and MAXIM dancing in evening wear. "I" looks at MAXIM longingly and happily—and he at her.

DISSOLVE TO:
INT. MRS. VAN HOPPER'S SUITE—DAY

The next day, in her suite, MRS. VAN HOPPER is seated in a chair, wearing a rather loud dressing gown while her bed is being made. The door opens, and "I" comes in, dressed in spotless white.

"I"

May I go now?

MRS. VAN HOPPER

For the number of lessons you've had, you ought to be ready for Wimbledon. But this will be your last . . . so make the most of it. The trouble is, with me laid up like this, you haven't had enough to do. But I'm getting rid of that nurse today, and from now on you'll stick to your job.

"I"'s expression becomes slightly desperate.

"I"

Yes, Mrs. Van Hopper.

She turns and goes.

MRS. VAN HOPPER

Nurse?

NURSE

Yes?

MRS. VAN HOPPER

Are you absolutely *sure* you left those messages for Mr. de Winter?

• 19 •

NURSE

Why, yes, Madame.

MRS. VAN HOPPER

I simply can't believe it. He would most certainly have called me back. Oh, well, poor boy, I simply hate to see him so alone.

DISSOLVE TO:
PICTURESQUE SECTION OF
CORNICHE ROAD—LONG SHOT—DAY

On the corniche road, MAXIM's car is running at a comfortable pace. MAXIM has an expression of calm contentment. "I" looks at him shyly, wistfully.

"I"

I wish there could be an invention that bottled up a memory, like perfume. And it never faded, and it never got stale. And I could uncork the bottle any time I pleased, and live the moment all over again.

MAXIM

And what particular moment in your young life would you want to keep?

"I" *(embarrassed)*

Oh, all of them—from these past few days. I think I've collected a whole shelf full of bottles.

MAXIM *(gravely)*

Sometimes, you know, those little bottles contain demons that pop out at you just when you're trying most desperately to forget.

"I" is considerably let down, having gone so far as to practically declare her love. MAXIM turns and looks at her, sees that she is depressed and that her mood is changed.

He looks away and steps on the gas. The car gathers speed. There is a few moments' silence. "I" looks at him nervously out of the corner of her eyes and starts biting her nails.

MAXIM *(looking at her)*
Stop biting your nails!

There is another moment's silence while "I" broods, embarrassed, and then she blurts out:

"I"
I wish I were a woman of thirty-six, dressed in black
satin, with a string of pearls.

MAXIM
You wouldn't be here with me if you were.

She puts her hands in her lap. She seems close to tears. Suddenly she turns and speaks sharply:

"I" *(passionately)*
Will you please tell me, Mr. de Winter . . . why do you
ask me to come out with you? Oh—it's obvious that
you want to be kind—
    but why choose me for your charity?

MAXIM stops the car and turns on her.

MAXIM
I asked you to come out with me because I wanted
your company. You've blotted out the past for me more
than all the bright lights of Monte Carlo. But if you

think I'm just being charitable or kind, you can leave the car now and find your own way home! Go on, open the door and get out!

He looks at her. Her face is averted. Tears have started from her eyes. He looks back ahead. Suddenly he reaches in his pocket, pulls out his handkerchief, tosses it into her lap.

MAXIM

Here. Blow your nose.

She uses the handkerchief, blowing her nose hard.

MAXIM

Please don't call me Mr. de Winter. I have a very impressive array of first names—George Fortescue Maximilian. You needn't bother with all of them at once. My family call me Maxim.

She looks at him. He is certainly the most unpredictable person she has ever encountered.

MAXIM

And another thing—I want you to promise me never to wear black satin, or pearls, or to be thirty-six years old.

"I" (smiles)

Yes—MAXIM . . .

MAXIM kisses his finger and places it affectionately on her forehead.

FADE IN:
INT. "I'S" BEDROOM—MORNING

We see a flower box on a table, with a note saying "Thank you for yesterday—MAXIM." "I" is humming happily, arranging MAXIM's white flowers in a vase on the same table.

Suddenly, she hears MRS. VAN HOPPER let out a scream.

MRS. VAN HOPPER

For the love of Pete! Come here!

"I" hurries into the next room.

INT. MRS. VAN HOPPER'S ROOM

MRS. VAN HOPPER is in bed, smoking a cigarette, an open cable in her hand as "I" comes in. Her breakfast tray is still by her bed.

MRS. VAN HOPPER

What do you think! My daughter's engaged to be married!

"I"

Really? I'm so glad.

MRS. VAN HOPPER jumps out of bed and slips into her robe.

MRS. VAN HOPPER

We must leave for New York at once. Get reservations on the *Aquitania*, and we'll take the 12:30 train for Cherbourg. Hurry up!

"I" is crestfallen. MRS. VAN HOPPER, now putting on her slippers, notices her look.

Hurry up! We have no time to waste, and don't dawdle! Hurry up and got a maid in to help us with the packing! We've no time to waste. Go on—and don't dawdle!

"I" goes swiftly from the room and turns into the door to her own room. "I" comes to the bedside telephone and, lifting the receiver hurriedly, speaks quickly and quietly:

> **"I"**
>
> Mr. de Winter, please.

Her face falls.

> **"I"**
>
> He's gone out and won't be back till noon? Oh. Give me the porter, please.

DISSOLVE TO:
INT. MRS. VAN HOPPER'S SUITE—
SEMI LONG SHOT—DAY

A close-up of a clock that is about to strike twelve o'clock. Then, in MRS. VAN HOPPER's suite, we see "I," dressed in her hat and coat, with her bag in one hand, standing apart from MRS. VAN HOPPER, looking very miserable. She turns suddenly to her employer.

> **"I"**
>
> I'll go and see if anything's left in my room.

She hurries out of the door.

INT. "I'S" BEDROOM—
SEMI CLOSE UP—DAY

"I" hurries into the room and over to the telephone, saying very quietly:

"I"

Has Mr. de Winter come in yet? Oh, he has? Would you connect me, please?

INT. MRS. VAN HOPPER'S SUITE—
SEMI LONG SHOT—DAY

MRS. VAN HOPPER looks around impatiently, then comes out into the lobby and toward "I"'s room.

INT. "I'S" BEDROOM—
SEMI LONG SHOT—DAY

As MRS. VAN HOPPER enters the room, "I" springs away from the phone guiltily. MRS. VAN HOPPER looks at her suspiciously.

"I"

I'm trying to find a book—I must have packed it.

MRS. VAN HOPPER

Well, come on . . . the car's waiting at the door.

She turns to go, and "I" follows unwillingly. As she leaves, the phone starts to ring, unheard.

DISSOLVE TO:
EXT. HOTEL DE PARIS—
SEMI CLOSE UP—DAY

Outside the hotel the hand luggage is being loaded into a car.

• 25 •

EXT. HOTEL DE PARIS—
SEMI CLOSE UP

"I" gives a final despairing look back into the hotel. Then with sudden decision, she turns to MRS. VAN HOPPER:

"I"

I want to leave a forwarding address—in case they happen to find that book.

She has leapt up the steps almost before she has finished speaking. MRS. VAN HOPPER opens her mouth to speak angrily, but the girl is gone.

INT. HOTEL DESK—
SEMI CLOSE UP—DAY

"I" is speaking to the CONCIERGE.

"I"

Would you ring Mr. de Winter, please?

CONCIERGE

Oui, Madame. (into the phone) Cent quarante-deux.

INT. MAXIM'S BEDROOM—
SEMI LONG SHOT—DAY

In MAXIM's room, the telephone starts to ring. There is the loud sound of running water from the bathroom. We can hear MAXIM splashing and singing in the bathroom, sufficiently loud to make him fail to hear the telephone.

INT. HOTEL DESK

"I" waiting nervously while the CONCIERGE listens at the telephone. He puts down the phone and shakes his head.

CONCIERGE

There isn't any answer.

"I" turns away.

EXT. HOTEL DE PARIS—
SEMI CLOSE UP—DAY

MRS. VAN HOPPER in the car, expostulating with the PORTER.

MRS. VAN HOPPER

Tell her to hurry up!

PORTER

Yes, Madame.

INT. HOTEL LOBBY & DINING ROOM

"I" hurries across the lobby toward the dining room. She looks in, then quickly turns back into the lobby.

"I"

I'm looking for Mr. de Winter.

WAITER

Mr. de Winter just ordered breakfast in his room, Madame.

EXT. MAXIM'S SUITE—
CORRIDOR (3)—SEMI CLOSE UP—DAY

"I" breathlessly arriving at the door of MAXIM's room. She knocks.

MAXIM'S VOICE

Come in.

She opens the door and is in the little foyer leading to the sitting room. (Beyond are MAXIM's bedroom and bathroom.)

INT. MAXIM'S BEDROOM—
SEMI CLOSE UP—DAY

MAXIM stands in the half-open door of the bathroom, attired in trousers and dressing gown, his face still lathered from shaving. He looks in astonishment as he sees who it is and comes toward "I."

MAXIM *(wiping the remaining lather from his face)*
Hello. What are you doing here? Anything the matter?

SEMI LONG SHOT—SITTING ROOM

"I" advances further into the sitting room and stands awkwardly.

"I"
I've come to say good-bye . . . We're going away.

MAXIM
What on earth are you talking about?

"I" **(coming to him)**
It's true. We're going now. I was afraid I wouldn't see you again.

MAXIM
Where's she taking you to?

"I"
New York—and I don't want to go. I shall hate it. I shall be miserable.

MAXIM turns to go back into the bathroom, picking up his clothes from a nearby chair.

MAXIM

I'll dress in here. I shan't be long.

He goes back to the bathroom, leaving the door half open.

SEMI LONG SHOT

"I" stands a lonely figure in the middle of the room. There is a pause. Then we hear MAXIM's voice from the bathroom.

MAXIM'S VOICE

Which would you prefer, New York or Manderley?

"I" *(calling back appealingly)*

Please don't joke about it . . . Mrs. Van Hopper's waiting . . . I'd better say good-bye now.
(she looks around nervously, worried about the time)

MAXIM'S VOICE

I'll repeat what I said—either you go to America with Mrs. Van Hopper or you come home to Manderley with me.

"I"

You mean you want a secretary or something?

MAXIM'S VOICE

I'm asking you to marry me, you little fool.

At this moment there is a knock on the outer door. MAXIM, his shirt now on, puts his head out of the bathroom door beyond and calls:

MAXIM

Come in.

The waiter enters, wheeling the table and breakfast.

MAXIM

Is that my food? I'm famished. I haven't had any breakfast.

There is a long silence while he lays the breakfast out and pulls up a chair. Eventually he goes out of the room. "I" still stands helplessly in the middle of the room. The bathroom door opens, and MAXIM emerges, putting on his coat. He comes through the bedroom and toward the table.

SEMI CLOSE UP

MAXIM sits at the table and motions "I" to a seat. He starts to spread butter on a piece of toast, and as he proceeds to eat it, speaks:

MAXIM

My suggestion doesn't seem to have gone at all well— I'm sorry.

"I"

But you don't understand . . . I'm not the sort of person men marry.

MAXIM

What on earth do you mean?

"I"

I don't belong in your sort of world, for one thing.

MAXIM *(laughs a little)*

What *is* my sort of world?

"I"

Well—Manderley—you know what I mean.

MAXIM

I'm the best judge of whether you belong there or not. Of course, if you don't love me, that's different. A fine blow to my conceit, that's all.

"I" *(desperately)*

Oh, I do love you! I love you most dreadfully. I've been crying all morning because I thought I'd never see you again.

He laughs and stretches a hand out across the table to her.

MAXIM

Bless you for that . . . I'll remind you of this one day. You won't believe me. It's a pity you have to grow up.

He starts to eat again, talks between mouthfuls of toast and sips of coffee.

MAXIM *(continuing)*

Now that's settled, you may pour me some more coffee. I take two lumps of sugar and milk. The same with my tea. Don't forget.

As "I" pours out the coffee, he continues:

MAXIM

Who's I going to break the news to Mrs. Van Hopper? Shall you, or shall I?

"I" *(still scarcely believing it)*
You—you tell her—she'll be so angry.

He pushes his plate away.

MAXIM

What's the number of her room?

"I"

She's not there. She's downstairs in the car.

He stretches out to the desk nearby and picks up the telephone.

MAXIM

Give me the desk, please.

(slight pause)

You'll find Mrs. Van Hopper waiting at the front entrance. Would ask her very kindly with my compliments if she could come up to see me in my room. Yes, in my room.

EXT. HOTEL DE PARIS—
SEMI LONG SHOT—DAY

INT. CAR—CLOSE UP—DAY

Outside the Hotel de Paris, the CONCIERGE comes up to MRS. VAN HOPPER's car.

CONCIERGE

Mr. de Winter asks you to come up to his room.

MRS. VAN HOPPER

Mr. de Winter? . . . Why certainly . . .

She starts to clamber out, assisted by the COMMISSIONAIRE and CLERK.

INT. MAXIM'S SITTING ROOM—
SEMI CLOSE UP—DAY

Back in MAXIM's room, he bends over "I" and with a hand on her shoulder says:

MAXIM

This isn't your idea of a proposal, is it? It ought to be in a conservatory—you in a white frock with a rose in your hand, and a violin playing in the distance—and I should be making violent love to you behind a palm tree.

"I" looks up at him a trifle self-consciously.

MAXIM

Poor darling—never mind.

"I" *(smiling happily)*

I *don't* mind.

There is a knock at the door.

MAXIM

Don't worry, don't worry. You won't have to say a word.

SEMI CLOSE UP

MAXIM holds open the door as MRS. VAN HOPPER comes in. Her face is wreathed in smiles. She is chattering rapidly.

MRS. VAN HOPPER

I'm so glad you called me, Mr. de Winter. I was making *such* a hasty departure. It was rude of me not to let you know, but a cable came this morning announcing that my daughter is engaged to be married . . .

MAXIM comes up beside her. "I" is in the background near the door.

MAXIM

That's rather a coincidence, Mrs. Van Hopper. I asked you up here in order to tell you of *my* engagement.

MRS. VAN HOPPER

You don't mean it! Well, how perfectly wonderful! How romantic. Who *is* the lucky lady?

MAXIM merely gestures toward "I." MRS. VAN HOPPER turns and looks. Her face presents a pretty picture of utter bewilderment.

MAXIM

I have to apologize for depriving you of your companion in this abrupt way. I hope it doesn't inconvenience you too greatly.

MRS. VAN HOPPER

When did all this happen?

"I"

Just now, Mrs. Van Hopper. Only a few minutes ago.

MRS. VAN HOPPER

I simply can't believe it!

(roguishly)

And I suppose I ought to scold you for not having breathed a word of this to me. What am I thinking of? I should give you both my congratulations and my blessings. I'm so *very* happy for you both! When and where is the wedding to be?

MAXIM

Here. As soon as possible.

MRS. VAN HOPPER

Whirlwind romance! Splendid! I can easily postpone my sailing for a week. This poor child has no mother, so I shall take responsibility for all the arrangements—the trousseau, the reception, everything! And I'll give the bride away.

But—my luggage!

(she wheels on "I" by force of habit)

Go down and tell the porter to take everything out of the car.

"I" seems about to obey, but MAXIM intervenes.

MAXIM

We're most grateful to you, Mrs. Van Hopper—but I think we both prefer to have it all as quiet as possible. I couldn't possibly allow you to change your sailing plans.

MRS. VAN HOPPER

But—

MAXIM

I'll have your luggage brought back.

Thank you, MAXIM. I'll be right down.

He looks into her eyes, sees she is no longer afraid to face MRS. VAN HOPPER, and goes. MRS. VAN HOPPER turns on "I" the minute MAXIM has gone, dropping all pretense.

MRS. VAN HOPPER

So this is what has been happening during my illness! Tennis lessons my foot!

(she goes close to "I")

I suppose I've to hand it to you for a fast worker. How did you manage it? Still waters certainly run deep! Tell me: have you been doing anything you shouldn't?

"I"

I don't know what you mean.

MRS. VAN HOPPER

Oh, well—never mind. I always did say that Englishmen have strange tastes. But you'll certainly have your work cut out as mistress of Manderley. To be perfectly frank with you, my dear, I can't see you doing it. You haven't the experience, you haven't the faintest idea what it means to be a great lady. Of course, you know why he's marrying you, don't you? You haven't flattered yourself that he's in love with you. The fact is, that empty house got on his nerves to such an extent he nearly went off his head. He just couldn't go on living alone.

"I"

You'd better leave, Mrs. Van Hopper. You'll miss your train.

MRS. VAN HOPPER turns and faces "I." A queer twisted smile crosses her face.

> **MRS. VAN HOPPER** *(with withering sarcasm)*
> Mrs. de Winter.
>
> *(with a sour laugh)*

Good-bye, my dear, and *good luck.*

FADE OUT.

FADE IN:
EXT. MONTE CARLO STREET—
LONG SHOT—DAY

In the foreground of a Monte Carlo street stands MAXIM's car—empty. It is a fairly busy market street. A flight of steps leads up to a stone building. A sign on the building says, "*MAIRIE: SALLE DES MARIAGES*" ("Mayoralty: room for marriages.")

From the entrance come MAXIM and "I." They walk down the steps. The MAYOR leans out of one window and calls, excitedly:

> **MAYOR**
> Monsieur! Vous avez oublié votre carnet de mariage!

> **"I"**
> What is he saying?

> **MAXIM** *(laughing)*
> I forgot the proof that we're married!

The MAYOR lets the certificate fly, and it flutters down to MAXIM.

MAXIM

Ahh. Somebody else had the same idea.

Near the foot of the steps, where MAXIM and "I" are standing, a noisy crowd of children and townspeople run into the picture, followed by a wedding group. The bride is in white and carries a sheaf of lilies. MAXIM and "I" look at the new wedding party.

"I" *(wistfully)*

Isn't she sweet?

MAXIM *(giving her a quick look)*

You'd have liked a bridal veil, or at least a bouquet, wouldn't you!

"I" doesn't answer. MAXIM looks at her and realizes he has been right. MAXIM goes over to the flower seller, and pulling a handful of notes from his pocket, takes a huge bouquet, which he presents to "I."

"I"

Oh, Max, how lovely! How perfectly lovely!

DISSOLVE TO:
EXT. FRENCH STREET—
SEMI LONG SHOT—DAY

We see the car speed away up the long, rising, cobbled street.

FADE OUT.

FADE IN:
EXT. MANDERIEY GATES—
CLOSE UP—DAY

Worked into the wrought-iron scroll work of a pair of big gates, is the word, "MANDERLEY."

EXT. LARGE GATES—
SEMI LONG SHOT – DAY

MAXIM and "I," seated in an open car, drive up to the opening gates of Manderley. The car slows down and continues through a Gothic arch. The car rounds the bend. Ahead is a long, gloomy stretch and another bend.

TWO SHOT—"I" & MAXIM IN THE CAR
PLATE ALREADY SHOT

"I" is looking ahead, nervously. She suddenly shivers with a strange apprehension. MAXIM looks at her.

MAXIM

Cold, darling?

"I" *(with a tremulous smile)*
Yes. Just a little bit.

MAXIM

No need to be frightened, you know. You've only got to be yourself and they'll all adore you. And you don't have to worry about the house—Mrs. Danvers is the housekeeper. Just leave it to her.

The length of this drive is oppressive. "I" thinks that beyond each bend she will see the house. MAXIM, with a slight frown, looks up at the sky.

MAXIM

Hello . . . started to rain.

Big raindrops begin to descend. "I" pulls a mackintosh from the back. The rain increases.

MAXIM

We'd better hurry up.

We hear the car increase in speed.

EXT. DRIVE (2d UNIT)—
LONG SHOT & ANGLE OVER
BONNET OF CAR—RAIN

Over their shoulders we see the hood of the car approaching another bend, and then another. At length the car turns a sharp bend and there, suddenly, is the house. The rain is now falling in torrents, but it cannot conceal the imposing building.

CLOSE TWO SHOT—"I" AND
MAXIM IN CAR—RAIN
PLATE ALREADY SHOT

MAXIM turns to "I," smiles, and waves his hand toward the house.

MAXIM

That's it! That's Manderley!

As the car comes to a standstill in front of the house, we see a butler and footman waiting on the steps.

EXT. MANDERLEY—
SEMI LONG SHOT—DAY

FRITH, the butler, comes running down the steps with an umbrella. MAXIM and "I" rush out under the umbrella held by FRITH.

EXT. MANDERLEY—
SEMI CLOSE UP—DAY

As they mount the steps, MAXIM says:

MAXIM

Here we are, Frith. Everyone well?

FRITH

Yes, sir. Thank you, sir. I'm glad to see you home, sir. I hope you've been keeping well.

MAXIM

This is Mrs. de Winter, Frith.

"I," with wet wisps of hair hanging down her face, shyly puts out her hand to FRITH.

"I"

How do you do?

FRITH gives a little bow, then sees the outstretched hand, and takes it.

INT. HALL—SEMI LONG SHOT—DAY
SHOT FROM BEHIND THEM.

As they enter the hall and FRITH removes the umbrella, MAXIM stops. Beyond them we see about twenty servants lined up in a semicircle.

MAXIM (annoyed)

I didn't expect the whole staff to be in attendance.

During this "I" has been pulling the mackintosh from her head. Her hair has been flattened by it, and wisps of hair have got wet and hang down her face. FRITH replies to MAXIM in a low voice.

FRITH

Mrs. Danvers' orders, sir.

MAXIM

(without expression)
Oh.

He turns to "I," from whom FRITH is taking the mackintosh.

MAXIM

I'm sorry about this, but it won't take long.

They turn towards the group of waiting servants and start to go towards them.

LONG SHOT

We get the impression of a tableau with MAXIM guiding "I" towards the group. The hall is vast, with its minstrel gallery and broad sweeping staircase.

SEMI CLOSE UP

"I" goes towards the group; rain still drips down her cheeks from the front of her hair. "I" is piloted towards the group of waiting servants by MAXIM. We see the shyness overcoming her as she advances.

Almost as though from nowhere, the figure of a tall, gaunt woman steps into the side of the picture and advances.

MAXIM

This is Mrs. Danvers.

MRS. DANVERS (coldly to "I")

How do you do, Madam. I have everything in readiness for you.

"I"

Oh, . . . that's good of you, I'm sure. I didn't expect . . . anything.

She is playing with her glove in her nervousness and drops it.

MAXIM

We'd like some tea, Frith.

FRITH

It's ready in the library, sir.

MRS. DANVERS stoops to pick up "I"'s glove. She hands it to her with the faintest trace of a smile of scorn. "I" is very unhappy. MRS. DANVERS looks her straight in the eye. "I" cannot bear her look and lowers her eyes.

MAXIM

Come along, darling.

As "I" steals a look at MRS. DANVERS and turns away, the scorn on MRS. DANVERS' face increases slightly.

FADE OUT.

FADE IN:
INT. "I'S" SUITE—
LATE EVENING TWILIGHT

In "I"'s bedroom, thin streaks of light coming in from outside.

CLOSE SHOT

ALICE, the maid, is rather distastefully handling "I's" wet clothes.

"I" is seated at the dressing table, trying to do something with her lank hair. "I," furtively watching ALICE in the mirror, wishes she'd go. There is a knock at the door. "I" looks up eagerly.

"I"

Oh, MAXIM? Come in!

MED. SHOT—DOOR

The door opens and in comes MRS. DANVERS.

"I's" voice (*disappointed*)

Oh. Good evening, Mrs. Danvers.

MRS. DANVERS

Good evening, Madam.

MRS. DANVERS moves into the room. She glances at ALICE—a glance of dismissal. ALICE puts "I's" wet clothes over her arm, looks at Mrs. Danvers as much as to say "look at these rags," and goes.

MRS. DANVERS

I hope that Alice has been satisfactory, Madam?

"I"

Oh, yes, thank you—perfectly.

MRS. DANVERS

She's the parlor maid. She'll have to look after you until your own maid arrives.

"I"

But I haven't a maid. I'm sure Alice will do very nicely.

MRS. DANVERS *(coldly)*

I'm afraid that would not do for very long, Madam. It's usual for ladies in your position to have a personal maid.

CLOSE UP

"I" looking at MRS. DANVERS. She is unable to stand the steady, freezing gaze of this woman, and turns away, pretending to be busy with her face powder.

SEMI LONG SHOT

MRS. DANVERS goes over to inspect the arrangement of the beds.

MRS. DANVERS

I hope you approve the new decoration of these rooms, Madam.

"I"

Oh, I didn't know they'd been changed. I hope you didn't have to go to too much trouble.

MRS. DANVERS

I only followed Mr. de Winter's instructions.

"I"

What did it look like before?

MRS. DANVERS

It had an old paper and different hangings. It was never used much, except for occasional visitors.

"I"

Then it wasn't Mr. de Winter's room originally?

MRS. DANVERS

No, Madam. He has never used the *east* wing before.
Of course, there is no view of the sea from here.
 "I" is looking toward MRS. DANVERS.

MRS. DANVERS

The only good view of the sea is from the *west* wing.

"I"

The room is very charming, and I'm sure I shall be
comfortable.

There is a moment's silence. "I" doesn't know what to do with
herself, picks up her brushes again.

SEMI LONG SHOT

MRS. DANVERS turning from window and coming back to "I."

MRS. DANVERS

If there is anything you want done, Madam, you have
only to tell me.

"I"

I suppose you've been at Manderley for many years—
longer than anyone else?

MRS. DANVERS

Not so long as Frith. He was here when the old gentleman was living—when Mr. de Winter was a boy.

"I"

And you didn't come until after that?

MRS. DANVERS

I came here when the first Mrs. de Winter was a bride.

CLOSE UP

"I" looks away sharply. For a second we see the effect of the words on her face; then with an effort she summons her courage and swinging round in her chair, faces MRS. DANVERS directly.

"I"

Mrs. Danvers, I hope we shall be friends. You must be patient with me. This sort of life is new to me. And I do want to make a success of it and make Mr. de Winter happy. I know I can leave all the household arrangements to you.

MRS. DANVERS (coldly)

Very well. I hope I shall do everything to your satisfaction, Madam. I've managed the house since Mrs. de Winter's death, and Mr. de Winter has never complained.

MRS. DANVERS turns to leave but stops at the door and glares back at "I."

"I"

I—I think I'll go downstairs now.

INT. HALL—SEMI LONG SHOT

Along the long passage, MRS. DANVERS and "I" go toward the stairs.

• 47 •

SEMI CLOSE UP

As they reach the top of the stairs, MRS. DANVERS pauses and points to a door along the broad passage on the other side of the stairs.

MRS. DANVERS

The room in the west wing I was telling you about is there—through that door. It's not used now. It's the most beautiful room in the house—the only one that looks down across the lawns to the sea. *It was Mrs. de Winter's room.*

"I" hesitates while looking at the door. She turns and sees MRS. DANVERS' eyes fixed on her. MRS. DANVERS turns and moves swiftly out of picture. "I" glances back toward the door.

SEMI LONG SHOT

Over "I's" shoulder we see the mysterious door. Then we see lying against the foot of it, Rebecca's dog, JASPER.

FADE OUT.

FADE IN:
INT. DINING ROOM—NIGHT

CentEred in the foreground, on a place setting, is a napkin bearing the monogram: "R de W." Then we see "I" removing it and placing it on her lap. Then we see the whole dining table, with MAXIM at the head, unfolding his napkin, with FRITH and ROBERT, the footman, removing the service plates and preparing to serve the soup.

FADE OUT.

FADE IN:
EXT. MANDERLEY—LONG SHOT—DAY

A long view of Manderley in the early morning. It is a beautiful, sunny, peaceful day.

DISSOLVE TO:
INT. DINING ROOM—LONG SHOT—DAY

"I" comes into the dining room carrying her handbag, just as she did in the hotel. She is surprised to see a stranger seated at the table, near MAXIM's place. It is FRANK CRAWLEY. He has a great many letters and papers before him, which he is sorting out. He jumps to his feet as he sees "I."

FRANK *(awkwardly and shyly)*

Good morning.

"I"

Good morning.

FRANK

You're Mrs. de Winter, aren't you?

"I"

Yes.

FRANK *(embarrassed)*

My name is Crawley. I manage the estate for Maxim.

(pause)

I'm awfully glad to meet you.
    Fearful lot of stuff piled up while Maxim was away.

"I"

Yes, I'm sure there must have been.

• **49** •

(Another embarrassed pause)

I do wish I could help with some of it.

SEMI CLOSE UP—DINING ROOM DOOR

MAXIM has come in, carrying some letters. He has heard "I's"
remark.

MAXIM

Oh, no. Frank won't allow anyone to help him. He's
like an old mother hen with all his bills and rents and
taxes. Well, come on, Frank. We must go over these
estimates.

FRANK

I'll get my papers.

FRANK goes out of scene to gather up the papers.

SEMI CLOSE UP

MAXIM

You'll find quantities of breakfast over there, on the
sideboard. You must eat it all, or cook will be mortally
offended.

"I" *(smiling)*

I'll do my best, MAXIM.

MAXIM

I have to go over the place with Frank to make sure he
hasn't lost any of it. But you'll be all right, won't you?
Getting acquainted with your new home.

MAXIM gives her a quick, perfunctory kiss on the forehead
and turns and goes.

MAXIM

Have a look at *The Times*. There's a thrilling article on what's the matter with English cricket.

MEDIUM SHOT

As MAXIM and FRANK go to the door, MAXIM turns.

MAXIM

Oh—I forgot to tell you—my sister, Beatrice, and her husband, Giles Lacy, have invited themselves over for lunch.

"I"

Today?

SEMI CLOSE UP

MAXIM

Yes. I suppose the old girl can't wait to look you over. You'll find her very direct. If she doesn't like you, she'll probably tell you so to your face.

Don't worry, darling—I'll be back in time to protect you from her. Good-bye, darling.

"I"

Goodbye, Maxim.

SEMI CLOSE UP

"I" lifts the lids of the numerous covered dishes on the side-board. There are eggs, bacon, sausages, kedgeree, kippers, haddock, kidneys, oatmeal—and great sides of cold meats. The sight of so much food destroys whatever appetite she may have had. She pours herself a cup of tea and takes it to her lonely place at the end of the great table.

FRITH and ROBERT enter. ROBERT goes to the sideboard, FRITH to "I."

FRITH

Good morning, Madam.

"I"

Good morning, Frith.

FRITH crosses to the side table, glances at the covered dishes, undisturbed, then turns again to "I."

FRITH

Isn't there anything I could get for you, Madam?

"I" is drinking her tea.

"I"

No thank you. Really, I'm not hungry.

"I" puts down her cup, rises, and starts to go.

FRITH

The papers, Madam.

ROBERT has picked them up and handed them to her.

"I"

Oh—thank you.

She takes the papers and starts to the door. As she comes near it, she slips on the polished floor, almost falls.

MEDIUM SHOT

FRITH rushes forward to catch her. The camera swings with them as they come up to her.

"I" *(lamely)*

I—I slipped.

She goes into the great hall. FRITH steadies her for a few steps, guiding her by the arm.

"I"

Thank you, Frith.

She looks about the hall.

"I"

It's very big, isn't it?

Frith

Yes, madam—Manderley *is* a big place. This was the banquet hall in the old days. It's still used on great occasions, such as a big dinner or ball, and the public is admitted here, you know, once a week.

"I"

That's nice.

She walks on, unable to think of anything better to say.

INT. LIBRARY—
SEMI LONG SHOT—DAY

In the library, the windows are wide open and the curtains blowing. "I" enters and gives a shiver. She crosses to the windows, looks out. Masses of clouds are blowing up from over the sea, covering the sun. She closes the windows, goes to the fireplace, looks about for matches.

LIBRARY DOOR

FRITH appears in the doorway.

FRITH

    I beg pardon, madam.

CLOSE UP

"I" turns quickly, guiltily. She feels she's been caught doing something she shouldn't.

FRITH

    I wished to say, madam, that the fire is not usually lit
    in the library until the afternoon.
    But you will find one in the morning room. Of course,
    if you wish this fire lit now, madam . . .

"I"

Oh, no—I wouldn't dream of it. Thank you, Frith.

FRITH

Mrs. de Winter—(he hesitates, fearing that he has been tactless)—I mean, the late Mrs. de Winter—always did her correspondence and telephoning in the morning room after breakfast.

"I"

Thank you, Frith.

She turns and goes back towards the hall.

INT. HALL—DAY—
SEMI CLOSE UP

Outside the dining room door, she takes a few steps, then pauses awkwardly.

FRITH

Is there anything wrong, madam?

"I" *(hesitating)*

No. Which way is the morning room?

FRITH

It's that door there, on the left.

SEMI LONG SHOT

FRITH in the foreground, "I's" small figure crosses the large hall.

INT. MORNING ROOM—
LONG SHOT—DAY

"I" comes into the small morning room. It is a bright and cheerful room, exquisitely furnished and obviously a woman's room by the quantities of flowers in it. There is a blazing fire, in front of which JASPER is lying. "I" shyly inspects the room.

SEMI CLOSE UP

JASPER gets up from before the fire and ambles out the room.

SEMI CLOSE UP

"I" does not notice the dog has gone. She behaves almost as though she were an intruder. She crosses to the writing desk, and begins to examine its contents, which include an address book, guest book, and menu book. She looks almost furtively about her. A slight sound from outside makes her start guiltily away, but after a moment she turns back.

CLOSE UP

She picks up an address book, and we see the initials "R de W." "I" lowers herself into the chair. Suddenly we hear a telephone ring.

"I" starts, and with her eyes still fixed on the open book, lifts the telephone hurriedly. She puts the receiver to her ear. She listens for a moment, and then apparently repeats what was said to her.

"I"

Mrs. de Winter? I'm afraid you've made a mistake. Mrs. de Winter has been dead for over a year.

As she starts to replace the receiver, she suddenly realizes her faux pas and exclaims:

"I"

Oh, I mean . . .

There is a slight sound behind her; she turns quickly and looks upwards.

MRS. DANVERS stands behind her chair, regarding her with expressionless eyes.

MRS. DANVERS

That was the house telephone, Madam. Probably the head gardener, wishing instructions.

"I" *(lamely)*

Did you want to see me, Mrs. Danvers?

MRS. DANVERS

Mr. de Winter has informed me that his sister, Beatrice Lacey, and Major Lacey are expected for luncheon. I'd like to know if you approve of the menu.

She bends over "I" and, picking up a menu from the desk, proffers it to her.

"I" *(without looking at it)*

Oh, I'm sure they're very suitable—very nice, indeed.

MRS. DANVERS

You will notice, Madam, that I left a blank space for the sauce. Mrs. de Winter was always most particular about sauces.

"I"

Oh . . . let's have whatever you think Mrs. de Winter would have ordered.

MRS. DANVERS prepares to withdraw. She looks steadily at "I" as she says:

MRS. DANVERS

Thank you, Madam. (as she goes she adds) When you have finished your letters, Madam, Robert will take them to the post.

"I"

My letters? Oh, yes, of course, Mrs. Danvers.

"I," feeling it incumbent on her to do some correspondence, hesitates, looks around, then opens the drawer at the left of the writing table. She takes out a sheet of the expensive note paper, puts it down on the desk and sits. She opens Rebecca's address book.

CLOSE UP

We see a page of address book from over "I's" shoulder. In Rebecca's handwriting we see several names:

> *Duchess of Atherton*
> *12 Wingate Place*
> *Sir Nigel Armbruster*
> *412 Landsdowne Road*
> *Marquis of Armingham*
> *3 Palace Court Lane*

"I" knocks over a china cupid on the desk. It falls to the floor and smashes. She hastily gathers up the pieces and stuffs them in the back of a desk drawer. Then she settles down again despondently in her chair.

FADE OUT.

INT. HALL—LONG SHOT—DAY

In the hall, GILES and BEATRICE are entering. FRITH is taking GILES' hat and BEATRICE 's cape.

BEATRICE
Hello, Frith.

FRITH
Good morning, Mrs. Lacy.

BEATRICE

Where's Mr. de Winter?

FRITH

I believe he went down to the farm with Mr. Crawley.

BEATRICE

How tiresome of him not to be here when we arrive—
and how typical!

During this we see "I" in foreground at the head of the stairs,
shrinking back into the shadows out of view as FRITH shows
GILES and BEATRICE into the library. JASPER looks up at
her and whines.

HALL LEADING TO LIBRARY—
MEDIUM SHOT AT DOOR

"I" comes into the scene and stops a few feet from the library
door, which is partially open. She stops to adjust her clothes a
little and gives a few frantic pats to her hair. She hears voices
from the library.

BEATRICE'S VOICE

I must say that old Danvers does keep the house looking lovely. She certainly learned that trick of arranging flowers from Rebecca.

GILES' VOICE

I wonder how she likes it now—being ordered about by
an ex-chorus girl.

BEATRICE'S VOICE

Now—where on earth did you get the idea she's an
ex-chorus girl?

GILES' VOICE

He picked her up in the South of France, didn't he?

BEATRICE'S VOICE

What if he did?

GILES' VOICE

Well—I mean to say—there you are.

"I" pushes open the door and goes in. GILES and BEATRICE stand up.

"I" (timidly)

How do you do—I'm MAXIM's wife.

For a moment they both stare at her, both obviously surprised, then BEATRICE starts forward.

BEATRICE (murmuring as she approaches)

How do you do?

SEMI CLOSE UP

BEATRICE goes close to "I" and subjects her to close scrutiny.

BEATRICE

Well—I must say—you're quite different from what I expected!

CLOSE UP

"I," upset as well as taken aback by BEATRICE's remark, shyly shakes the hand BEATRICE is holding out to her, as GILES adds an embarrassed—

GILES *(palpably lying)*

Don't be silly. She's exactly what I told you she'd be.

He also holds out his hand and shakes very firmly with "I," as he continues:

GILES

Well—er—er—how d'you like Manderley?

"I"

It's very beautiful, isn't it?

BEATRICE

And how are you getting along with Mrs. Danvers?

"I"

Well, I've never met anyone quite like her before. She's—er—

GILES

You mean she scares you—she's not exactly an oil painting, is she? (he laughs uproariously at his own joke)

BEATRICE

Giles, you're very much in the way here. Go somewhere else.

GILES *(coughing)*

I'll try to find Maxim, shall I?

GILES lingers.

BEATRICE

Giles . . .

GILES goes out.

"I" *(shyly)*

I—I—didn't mean to say anything against Mrs. Danvers.

BEATRICE

Oh, there's no need to be frightened of her. But I shouldn't have any more to do with her than you can help. Shall we sit down?

"I"

Oh, yes, yes—please.

BEATRICE

You see, she's bound to be insanely jealous at first and she must resent you bitterly.

"I" *(astonished)*

But why should she?

BEATRICE

Don't you know? I should have thought Maxim would have told you. She simply adored Rebecca!

We see "I" reacting to BEATRICE's statement.

DISSOLVE TO:
LONG SHOT

DINING ROOM

In the dining room, BEATRICE is on MAXIM's right, FRANK on his left. GILES is on "I"'s right.

ROBERT is offering a platter of meat and vegetables to BEATRICE. She puts some on her plate.

BEATRICE

How are you, Robert?

ROBERT

Quite well, thank you, Madam.

BEATRICE

Still having trouble with your teeth?

ROBERT *(embarrassed)*

Unfortunately yes, Madam.

BEATRICE

You must have them out—all of them! Wretched nuisances—teeth.

ROBERT

Thank you, Madam.

With a great air of cheeriness, GILES is making conversation with "I."

GILES

Do you hunt?

"I"

No—I'm afraid, I don't even ride.

GILES

Have to ride down here. We all do. Which do you ride— side-saddle or astride? Oh, I forgot—you don't, do you? You must! Nothing else to do down here.

BEATRICE

Maxim, When will you start having parties here like the old days?

MAXIM *(grimly)*

Haven't thought about it.

BEATRICE

But everyone's dying to see you and—

(she looks off toward "I").

MAXIM

I can imagine.

BEATRICE

What about having the masquerade ball again this summer?

BEATRICE calls down to "I."

BEATRICE

My dear, are you fond of dancing?

SEMI CLOSE UP—"I" AND GILES

"I"

I love it. But I'm not very good at it.

GILES

Do you rhumba?

"I"

I've never tried.

GILES

You must teach me.

(he turns to MAXIM)

I say, old boy—I've been trying to find out what your wife *does* do.

MAXIM *(smiles)*

She sketches a little.

GILES

Sketches! Not this modern stuff, oh? You know, picture of a lampshade upside down to represent a soul in torment.

You don't—uh—you don't sail, do you?

"I" *(in a strained voice)*

No—I don't.

GILES

Thank goodness for that!

There is general consternation about the table. MAXIM stares grimly into space. BEATRICE glares at GILES as though she would slay him. GILES slaps his hand over his mouth.

Slowly the significance of what GILES has said begins to show on "I's" face. She flushes with embarrassment and looks down at her plate.

FADE OUT.

FADE IN:
INT. "I'S" BEDROOM—
SEMI CLOSE UP—DAY

In "I"'s bedroom, BEATRICE is adjusting her hat before the mirror. "I" is beside her.

BEATRICE

You're very much in love with Maxim, aren't you?

"I"

Why?

BEATRICE

I can see that you are . . .

Don't mind my saying so, but why don't you do something about your hair? Why don't you have it cut . . . or sweep it back behind your ears?

"I" holds her hair back behind her ears, turning her head for BEATRICE's inspection. The latter looks at her critically.

BEATRICE

No, that's worse. What does MAXIM say about it . . . Does he like it like that?

"I"

I don't know—he's never mentioned it.

BEATRICE

Oh, well—don't go by me. I can tell by the way you dress you don't care a hoot how you look. But I wonder Maxim hasn't been at you. He's so particular about clothes.

"I"

I don't believe he ever notices what I wear.

BEATRICE *(as they start out)*

He must have changed a lot, then . . .

INT. UPPER CORRIDOR—DAY

During this scene BEATRICE and "I" go to the stairs and down them, reaching a point in the lower hall near the large table.

BEATRICE

You mustn't worry about old Maxim—and his moods. One never knows what's going on in that quiet mind of his. Off he gets into a terrible rage—and when he *does!* But—I don't suppose he'll lose his temper with you. You seem such a placid little thing.

GILES' voice (from the front door)

Come *along*, old girl. We're supposed to be on the first tee at three o'clock.

BEATRICE

All right. I'm coming!

As they go out the front door, GILES says:

GILES

Goodbye, Maxim, old boy!

MAXIM

Goodbye, Giles. Thanks for coming, old boy.

EXT. MANDERLEY—
SEMI LONG SHOT—DAY

On the steps of the front entrance, MAXIM, "I," GILES, and BEATRICE emerge onto the steps. ROBERT stands near the door in the background. JASPER comes out too.
BEATRICE kisses "I" on the cheek.

BEATRICE

Well, goodbye, my dear. Forgive me for asking so many rude questions. We both really hope you'll be very happy.

"I" *(almost emotional in her hunger for kindness)*
Oh, thank you, Beatrice, thank you very much!

BEATRICE

And I must congratulate you on the way Maxim looks.
We were all very worried about him this time last year.
But, of course, you know the whole story.

DISSOLVE TO:

GILES and BEATRICE are just pulling away in a car, waving
good-bye. It disappears out of the picture for a moment and
then sweeps around the wide drive, away into the distance.

SEMI CLOSE UP

MAXIM takes a step or two down and looks up into the sky.

MAXIM

Thank heavens they're gone! Now, at last, we can have
a walk about the place. It looks like we might have a
shower—but you won't mind that, will you?

"I" *(happily)*
Of course not, Maxim. I'll go upstairs and get a coat.

MAXIM

There's a heap of mackintoshes in the flower room.

MAXIM goes up and steps inside the front door, calling inside.

MAXIM

Robert! Run and get a coat from the flower room for
Mrs. de Winter.

MAXIM comes back to "I."

What did you think of Beatrice?

"I"

I liked her very much. But she kept saying that I was
quite different from what she expected.

MAXIM

What the devil *did* she expect?

"I"

Someone much smarter, more sophisticated, I suppose.

(she pauses)

Do you like my hair?

MAXIM looks at her in astonishment.

MAXIM

Your hair? Of course I do. What's the matter with it?

"I"

Oh, nothing. I just wondered.

MAXIM *(looking at her)*
How funny you are.

ROBERT comes out from the house, carrying an oilskin coat.

"I"

Do I have to put it on?

MAXIM

Yes, certainly, certainly, certainly. Can't be too careful
with children.

MAXIM helps "I" into it, then says to JASPER:

> Come on, you lazy little beggar, and take some of that
> fat off.

SEMI LONG SHOT

They descend the steps and set out, arm in arm, across the
lawn, JASPER following at MAXIM's heels.

CLOSE UP—JASPER

As he follows behind them.

DISSOLVE TO:
2ND UNIT AS SHOT—EXT.
MANDERLEY—LONG SHOT—DAY

"I" and MAXIM are walking over the grounds away from the
house, JASPER with them.

EXT. LAWN—LONG SHOT.
2ND UNIT (L.S. AS SHOT)

EXT. NEAR TOP OF CLIFF—
WITH SEA BELOW

As they walk along, they come to a fork in the paths leading
down to the sea, and JASPER unhesitatingly runs ahead and
disappears down the path farthest to the right.

MAXIM

Jasper! Not that way! Come here!

JASPER starts to scamper down stairs which lead to the
beach.

CLOSE SHOT—MAXIM AND "I"
(AGAINST PLATE AS SHOT)

"I"

Where does that lead to?

MAXIM *(briefly)*

It leads to a small cove where we used to keep a boat.

"I"

Let's go down there.

MAXIM *(irritably)*

Well, no, It's just a dull and uninteresting stretch of sand—just like any other.

"I"

Oh, please . . .

MAXIM *(seeing her look of disappointment)*

All right . . . We'll walk down and take a look if you really want to.

2ND UNIT AS SHOT
LONG SHOT

"I" AND MAXIM start forward again.

2ND UNIT AS SHOT
LONG SHOT

"I" and MAXIM turn from the top of the palisades down onto the stairs leading to the beach, and walking down. JASPER runs ahead, barking.

"I" and MAXIM come down onto the beach. JASPER has disappeared, but they hear his bark from the other side of the rocks.

"I" (pointing)

That's Jasper!

(worried)

There may be something wrong—perhaps he's hurt himself.

MAXIM

He's all right. Leave him alone.

"I"

Don't you think I'd better go and see?

MAXIM (angrily)

Don't bother about him, I tell you. He can't come to any harm. He'll find his own way back.

But "I" has already left the picture. She starts clambering over rocks, calling out:

"I"

Jasper, Jasper! Oh, there you are!

"I" has reached the other side of the rocks and is now on a stretch of beach in a cove, hidden from MAXIM's view. This is a seminatural harbor created by the rocks jutting out into the sea. A mooring buoy is a little way out from the shore.

Shaded by the trees, which come down very nearly to the water's edge, is a small cottage. "I" stands a moment as she sees the reason for JASPER's barking.

JASPER is barking and leaping at the front door of the cottage, then lies down.

• 72 •

"I" comes up to him and crouches down.

"I"

Come on. What do you want in there? Let's go home.
Jasper, Jasper!

The door of the cottage slowly opens, revealing BEN, a man
dressed like a fisherman, with the face of an idiot. He peers
fearfully at "I," then looks down at JASPER.

"I"

I didn't know that there was anybody . . .

BEN

I know that dog. He comes from the 'ouse. He ain't
your'n.

"I"

No. He's Mr. de Winter's dog. Have you anything I
could tie him with?

BEN gapes open-mouthed at her. Suppressing her exaspera-
tion, she goes into the boathouse.

INT. INNER BOATHOUSE

In the boathouse, "I" enters a room completely furnished with
bookshelves, table, chairs, bed sofa, and a blanket with the
monogram "R de W." There are also ropes, sails, pots of paint,
and other paraphernalia. "I" looks round and finds a short
piece of thin rope. She picks it up and hurries out with it.

Outside, "I" ties up JASPER. In front of the cottage, BEN is
standing in a shadow in a corner.

BEN

Don't tell anyone you saw me in there, will you?

• 73 •

"I"

Don't you belong on the estate?

BEN

I wasn't doing nothin'. I was just putting me shells away.

She's gone in the sea, ain't she? She'll never come back no more.

CLOSE TWO SHOT—"I" AND BEN

"I"

No, she'll never come back. Come on, Jasper.

"I" climbs back onto the other section of beach toward where she had left MAXIM, with JASPER on his makeshift leash, to find it empty of MAXIM. She hurries, JASPER running ahead of her, to the stairs and up.

MAXIM sees "I" approach, turns and goes off. "I" runs into scene, breathless, calling after him.

"I"

Maxim! What's the matter? Maxim?

She starts out after, trying desperately to catch up with him.

"I"

I'm sorry I was such a time, but I had to find a rope for Jasper.

MAXIM strides forward silently at a still faster pace. The dog lags behind, delaying "I." MAXIM turns to look down at him.

MAXIM

Hurry up, Jasper, for heaven's sake!

"I"

Please wait for me. You look so angry!

MAXIM

You knew I didn't want you to go there—but you deliberately went.

"I"

Why not? There was only a cottage down there—and a strange man who was—

MAXIM

You didn't go *into* the cottage, did you?

"I"

Yes.

MAXIM *(interrupting)*

Don't go in there again! Do you hear?

"I"

Why not?

MAXIM

Because I hate the place—and if you had my memories, you wouldn't go there or talk about it or even think about it!

"I"

MAXIM, what's the matter? I'm sorry, darling! Please!

MAXIM

We ought to have stayed away. We should never have come back to Manderley! What a fool I was!

"I"

I've made you unhappy. Somehow I've hurt you. I can't bear to see you like this, because I love you so much.

MAXIM *(tensely, searching her face;*
takes her in his arms)

Do you? Do you?

He kisses her, then relaxes his hold.

Ah, I've made you cry . . . Forgive me—I sometimes seem to fly off the handle for no reason at all, don't I. Come: we'll go up and have some tea and forget all about it.

She smiles up at him through her tears.

"I"

Yes, let's forget all about it.

MAXIM

Here—let me have Jasper.

As she hands the leash to MAXIM, "I" automatically puts her hand in the pocket of the mackintosh, pulls out a handkerchief, and puts it to her eyes. She glances down at the handkerchief as she starts to return it to her pocket. The handkerchief is marked in the corner with a large embroidered initial "R." "I" stares down at the initial with a faraway look.

FADE OUT.

FADE IN:
INT. HALL—SEMI CLOSE UP—DAY

In the large hall, "I" seated with her legs curled under her on one of the window seats, looking thoughtfully out.

EXT. MANDERLEY—
SEMI LONG SHOT—DAY

INT. HALL—
SEMI CLOSE UP—DAY

"I" looks very disturbed. She turns away from the window, thinking hard.

SEMI CLOSE UP

"I" suddenly jumps to her feet and with a determined air crosses to the library.

INT. LIBRARY—
SEMI LONG SHOT—DAY

As she comes into the library, she sees FRANK CRAWLEY seated at a desk, immersed in his work.

INT. OFFICE—
SEMI LONG SHOT—DAY

As he sees "I" come in, FRANK stands up.

FRANK

Oh, hello, come in.

"I" *(as he rises)*

No, please don't get up, Mr. Crawley. I was wondering if you really meant what you said the other day about showing me the run of things?

FRANK

Of course I did.

"I"

What are you doing now?

FRANK

Notifying all the tenants that in celebration of Maxim's return with his bride, this week's rent will be free.

"I" *(greatly pleased)*

Was that Maxim's idea?

FRANK

Oh, yes! All the servants get an extra week's wages, too.

"I"

He didn't tell me. Can't I help you? I could at least lick the stamps.

FRANK *(weakly)*

That's terribly nice of you. Won't you sit down?

"I"

Oh, yes, thank you.

"I" sits down. He starts handing her envelopes as he addresses them. She licks the stamps and applies them as they talk.

"I" *(assuming a much too casual tone)*

I was down at the cottage on the beach the other day. There was a man there—a queer sort of person. Jasper kept barking at him.

FRANK

It must have been Ben. He's quite harmless. We give him odd jobs now and then.

                              "I"

That cottage place down there seemed to be going to
rack and ruin. Why isn't something done about it?

                            FRANK

I think if Maxim wanted anything done about it, he'd
tell me.

                              "I"

Are those all Rebecca's things down there?

                            FRANK

Yes, yes, they are.

                              "I"

What did she use the cottage for?

                            FRANK

The boat used to be moored near there.

                              "I"

What boat? What happened to it? Was that the boat
she was sailing in when she was drowned?

                            FRANK

Yes, it capsized and sank. She was washed overboard.

                              "I"

Wasn't she afraid to go out like that alone?

                            FRANK

She wasn't afraid of anything.

                              "I"
Where did they find her?

FRANK

Near Edgecoombe, about forty miles up channel—about two months afterwards. Maxim went up to identify her. It was horrible for him.

"I"

Yes, it must have been. Mr. Crawley, please don't think me too morbidly curious. It's just that I always feel myself at such a disadvantage—all the time. Whenever I meet anyone—Maxim's sister—even the servants—I know they're all thinking the same thing: they're all comparing me with—(she can't get the name out)—with—her—with Rebecca.

FRANK turns to her, very much concerned.

FRANK

You mustn't think that! For my part, I can't tell you how delighted I am that you married Maxim. It's going to make all the difference to his life . . . And from my point of view, it's very refreshing to find someone like yourself who is not entirely—in tune, shall we say, with Manderley.

"I" *(her eyes lowered)*

That's very sweet of you. I daresay I've been stupid, but every day, I realize the things that she had that I lack. Beauty and wit and intelligence and all the things that are so important.

FRANK

But you have qualities that are just as important—more important, if I may say so. Kindliness, sincerity, and—if you'll forgive me—modesty mean more to a husband than all the wit and beauty in the world. We none of us want to live in the past, Maxim least of all. It's up to you, you know, to lead us away from it.

                           "I"

I promise you I won't bring this up again, but before
we leave this conversation, would you answer just one
more question?

                         FRANK

If it's something I'm able to answer, I'll do my best.

                           "I"

Tell me. What was Rebecca really like?

          FRANK *(looks ahead reflectively*
                and answers slowly)

I suppose—I suppose she was the most beautiful crea-
ture I ever saw.

                      FADE OUT

                      CLOSE UP

We see a close-up of a fashion magazine: *Beauty: The Magazine for Smart Women*. As the pages turn, they stop on a black
gown with roses adorning the front, with the caption "For the
Gala Evening."

                      FADE IN:
          INT. MANDERLEY HALL—NIGHT

In the hall, "I" is clad in the same gown that we have just
seen in the magazine. She is very conscious of her clothes
and appearance, rather excited by them, but very nervous. She
goes into the library.

                           "I"

Good evening, Maxim.

CLOSE SHOT—MAXIM—
(HIS BACK TO CAMERA)

MAXIM *(without turning)*

Hello . . . The films of the honeymoon have arrived at last. Have we time for them before dinner?

On his last words, he turns and gradually is aware of her appearance. He looks at her. She walks in, affected and nervous.

MAXIM

What on earth have you done to yourself?

"I" *(casually)*

Oh, nothing . . . I just ordered a new dress from London . . . I hope you don't mind.

MAXIM

Oh, no. But do you think that sort of thing is right for you? It doesn't seem your type at all.

"I" *(very let down)*

Oh . . . I thought you'd like it.

MAXIM *(the cruel male!)*

And what have you done to your hair?

"I" doesn't answer. MAXIM sees he has hurt her, puts his arm around her.

Oh, I see, I see, I see... Oh, dear, well . . . never mind . . . You look lovely—lovely. It's very nice—for a change . . .

(dismissing the whole thing)

Shall we see these pictures?

"I" (very let down)

Yes, I'd love to see them.

MAXIM goes over and turns out the lights. The room is now lit only by the one lamp and the light from the projector. MAXIM is more or less lost in darkness. They watch the films with delight.

MAXIM

Look! Look! Look at you!

"I"

Wasn't that wonderful, darling? Can't we go back there sometime?

MAXIM

Yes, yes, of course! Ahh, look at you! There! Won't our grandchildren be delighted when they see how lovely you were!

"I"

Oh, look at you! Oh, I like that! Oh, remember that! Oh, I wish our honeymoon could have lasted forever, Maxim!

The film suddenly comes off the sprockets and breaks.

MAXIM

Oh, dash it! Oh, hang it! Threaded it up wrong as usual or something!

By this time the lights in the room are on. FRITH enters.

MAXIM

Yes, Frith, what is it?

FRITH

Excuse me, sir. May I have a word with you?

MAXIM

Yes, come in!

FRITH

It's about Robert, sir. There's been a slight unpleas-antness between him and Mrs. Danvers.

MAXIM

Oh, dear.

FRITH

Robert is very upset.

MAXIM

Well, this *is* trouble! What is it?

FRITH *(with a nervous cough)*

It appears that Mrs. Danvers has accused Robert of stealing a valuable ornament from the morning room. Robert denies the accusation most emphatically, sir.

MAXIM

What was the thing, anyway?

FRITH

The china cupid, sir.

MAXIM

Oh, dear, that's one of our treasures, isn't it? Well, tell Mrs. Danvers to get at the bottom of it, but tell her I'm sure that it wasn't Robert.

FRITH *(relieved)*

Very good, sir.

He exits. As soon as he has gone, MAXIM walks over toward the machine.

MAXIM

Why do they come to me with these things? That's your job, sweetheart.

"I"

Maxim . . . I wanted to tell you, but . . . but well, I forgot. The fact is . . . *I* broke the china cupid.

MAXIM *(very surprised)*

You broke it? Now why on earth didn't you say something about it when Frith was here?

"I"

I don't know. I didn't like to. I was afraid he would think me a fool.

MAXIM

He'll think you much more of a fool now. You'll have to explain to him and Mrs. Danvers.

"I"

Oh, no, Maxim! You do it! I'll go upstairs.

MAXIM *(very annoyed)*

Don't be such a little idiot, darling. Anyone would think you were afraid of them.

FRITH enters, ushering in MRS. DANVERS, who is obviously very angry.

MAXIM *(interrupting and obviously*
very annoyed with the whole thing)

It's all a mistake, Mrs. Danvers. Apparently Mrs. de Winter broke the cupid herself and forgot to say anything about it.

"I"

I'm so sorry. I never thought that I would get Robert would get into trouble.

MRS. DANVERS

Is it possible to repair the ornament, Madam?

"I"

No, I'm afraid it isn't. It smashed in pieces.

MAXIM

What did you do with the pieces?

"I"

I put them at the back of one of the drawers in the writing desk.

MAXIM

It looks as though Mrs. de Winter were afraid you were going to put her in prison, doesn't it, Mrs. Danvers? Well, never mind. Do what you can to find the pieces, see if they can be mended, and above all, tell Robert to dry his tears.

MRS. DANVERS

I will apologize to Robert, of course. Perhaps if such a thing happens again, Mrs. de Winter will tell me personally . . .

MAXIM *(interrupting impatiently)*

Yes, yes, all right, thank you, Mrs. Danvers. . .

MRS. DANVERS leaves the room. MAXIM goes about the business of repairing the film or of taking off the reel and putting in another, the scene continuing the while.

MAXIM

Well, I suppose that clip will hold all right, I don't know . . .

"I"

I'm awfully sorry, darling. It was very careless of me. Mrs. Danvers must be furious with me.

MAXIM

Hang Mrs. Danvers! Why on earth should you be frightened of her? You behave more like an upstairs maid or something, not like the mistress of the house at all.

"I"

I know I do. But I feel so uncomfortable . . . I try my best every day, but it's very difficult with people looking me up and down as if I were a prize cow.

MAXIM *(putting the film into the projector)*

What does it matter if they do? You must remember that life at Manderley is the only thing that interests anybody down here.

"I"

What a slap in the eye I must have been to them, then . . . I suppose that's why you married me . . . You knew I was dull and gauche and inexperienced, so there could never be any gossip about me.

MAXIM

Gossip! What do you mean?

"I"

I—I don't know. It was just something to say. Don't look at me like that! What's the matter? What have I said?

MAXIM turns off the projector.

MAXIM

It wasn't a very attractive thing to say, was it?

"I"

No. It was rude, hateful.

MAXIM (coldly)

I wonder if I did a very selfish thing in marrying you.

"I" (her voice almost a hoarse whisper, with fright)

How do you mean?

MAXIM

I'm not much of a companion to you, am I? You don't get much fun, do you? You ought to have married a boy, someone of your own age . . .

"I" (interrupting)

Oh, MAXIM, why do you say this? Of course we're companions.

MAXIM

Are we? I don't know. I'm very difficult to live with.

"I" *(eagerly)*

You're not difficult! You're easy, very easy. Our marriage is a success, isn't it—a great success!

*(He doesn't answer. She continues,
pleading, desperate)*

We're happy, aren't we? Terribly happy?

He still doesn't answer, and his failure to answer is a terrible blow to "I." She goes to him.

"I"

If you don't think we are happy, it would be much better if you didn't pretend. I'll go away. Why don't you answer me?

MAXIM

How can I answer you when I don't know the answer myself? If you say we're happy, let's leave it at that. Happiness is something I know nothing about.

MAXIM starts the projector. On the screen appear some films of the happy smiling faces of MAXIM and "I."

MAXIM'S VOICE

Look. There's the one when I left the camera on the tripod. Remember?

We see on the screen MAXIM's and "I"'s laughing faces.

FADE OUT.

FADE IN:

Close-up of a letter that reads: "Have gone up to London on some business of the estate. I shall return before evening, and certainly this brief holiday from me should be welcome. Maxim."

DISSOLVE TO:
INT. MORNING ROOM—
SEMI CLOSE UP—DAY

"I" is standing gazing unhappily at a glass case of china. Her mind is obviously occupied with thoughts of Rebecca. She has been crying, and we can still see traces of her tears. HILDA, the parlour maid, enters bringing in afternoon tea.

HILDA

Pardon me, Madam. Is there anything I can do for you?

"I"

I'm all right. Thank you very much.

HILDA

I'll bring the sandwiches immediately, Madam.

HILDA leaves. "I" goes to the window and looks out. She sees the west wing, with the figure of MRS. DANVERS moving about, closing a window.
HILDA reenters.

"I"

Hilda. The west wing. Nobody ever uses it anymore, do they?

HILDA

No. Madam. Not since the death of Mrs. de Winter.

"I" goes out into the main hall and hears voices above. JASPER comes running.

MRS. DANVERS' VOICE

Come along, Mr. Jack, or someone may see you.

FAVELL'S VOICE

Well, Danny, old harpy, it's been good to see you again. Makes me feel so breathless to pick up all the news.

JASPER starts to bark.

MRS. DANVERS' VOICE

I really don't think it's wise for you to come here, Mr. Jack.

JASPER continues to bark.

"I"

Jasper, come here!

FAVELL'S VOICE

Nonsense, nonsense. It's just like coming back home.

MRS. DANVERS' VOICE

Why, Mr. Jack . . .

FAVELL'S VOICE

Yes, and we must be careful not to shock Cinderella, mustn't we?

MRS. DANVERS' VOICE

If you leave through the garden door, she won't see you.

FAVELL'S VOICE

I must say I feel a little like a poor relation, sneaking around through back doors. Well, toodle-oo, Danny.

MRS. DANVERS' VOICE

Goodbye, Mr. Jack. And please be careful.

JASPER starts to whine.

"I"

Jasper, be quiet, be quiet.

FAVELL

Looking for me?

"I" turns around and is startled to see FAVELL through a wide-open window.

FAVELL

Hope I didn't make you jump, did I?

"I"

No, no, of course not. I didn't quite know who it was.

JASPER leaps up to the window, wagging his tail at FAVELL, who pats him affectionately.

FAVELL

Yes, you're pleased to see me, old boy. I'm glad there's someone in the family to welcome me back to Manderley. And how is dear old Max?

"I"

Very well, thank you.

FAVELL

I hear he went up to London, leaving his little bride all alone. Too bad. Isn't he rather afraid that someone might come down and carry you off?

MRS. DANVERS suddenly enters, looking extremely severe.

FAVELL

Danny, all your precautions were in vain. The mistress of the house was hiding behind the door. Oh, what about presenting me to the bride?

MRS. DANVERS

This is Mr. Favell, Madam.

"I"

How do you do?

FAVELL leaps through the window into the room and grasps "I" eagerly by the hand.

FAVELL

How do you do?

"I"

Won't you have some tea or something?

FAVELL

Well, now, isn't that a charming invitation? I've been asked to stay to tea, Danny, and I have a mind to accept.

MRS. DANVERS glares at FAVELL.

FAVELL

Oh, well, perhaps you're right. It's a pity, just when we were getting on so nicely. We mustn't lead the young bride astray, must we, Jasper?

JASPER looks up at FAVELL, wagging his tail.

FAVELL

Goodbye. It's been fun meeting you. Oh, and by the way, it would be very decent of you if you didn't mention this little visit to your revered husband. He doesn't exactly approve of me.

"I"

Very well.

FAVELL

That's very sporting of you. I wish I had a young bride of three months waiting for me at home. I'm just a lonely old bachelor. Fare thee well—ook!

FAVELL leaps awkwardly out the window.

FAVELL

Oh, and I know what was wrong with that introduction. Danny didn't tell you, did she? I am Rebecca's favorite cousin. Toodle-oo!

THE EMPTY ROOM—
FROM "I'S" VIEWPOINT

MRS. DANVERS has disappeared.

CLOSE UP

"I" comes to a sudden decision. She determinedly starts out of the room into the hall.

INT. HALL—
SEMI LONG SHOT—DAY

"I" starts to ascend the stairs.

INT. CORRIDOR—
SEMI LONG SHOT—DAY

"I" goes directly toward the door of Rebecca's big room.

SEMI CLOSE UP

She glances round almost furtively as she starts to turn the handle. She holds herself in a tense attitude when the wood makes a sound of crackling as it swings on its hinges. Opening it the minimum amount of space, she almost sidles in.

INT. REBECCA'S ROOM—
LONG SHOT—DAY

Inside the room it is practically dark. Just the vague shapes of furniture can be seen lit from the slightly open door through which "I" has come. We see her figure cross toward the window. She raises her hand and with sudden resolve pulls the cord which parts the curtains.

The flood of daylight reveals an astonishing scene. "I" swings round amazed, as she sees a most elegantly furnished room, expressed in the lightest possible tones—white predominates nearly everywhere. The four-poster bed is very regal on its double-stepped dais. The bed is made up with the coverlet folded back. A large spray of lovely fresh white flowers is set in a prominent position. There is also an ornate dressing table complete with brushes, combs, mirrors, and elaborate bottles of perfume. "I" approaches it, but is startled to see a large photo of MAXIM. She moves one of the brushes.

CLOSE UP

"I" gazes spellbound as her eyes begin to take in more details of the room.

SEMI CLOSE UP

Suddenly there is a sharp rap as the window blows open.
    The window slams open.

MRS. DANVERS' VOICE
Do you wish anything, Madam?

She looks up as MRS. DANVERS comes through the doorway. MRS. DANVERS stops short as she sees "I." There is a flash in her eyes—a flash of triumph. "I" stands by the bed, entirely confused. She puts a hand behind her back almost like a guilty child and half lowers her eyes. Then looking up she swallows slightly and says timidly:

"I"
I—I didn't expect to see you, Mrs. Danvers. I noticed one of the windows wasn't closed and I came up to see if I could fasten it.

MRS. DANVERS
Why did you say that? I closed it before I left the room. You opened it yourself, didn't you?

MRS. DANVERS goes to the open window and, in a business-like way, she closes it, shutting out the sound of the sea. She turns with her back to the windows and faces "I" who has come to the foot of the bed.

MRS. DANVERS

You've always wanted to see this room, haven't you, Madam? Why did you never ask me to show it to you? I was ready to show it to you every day.

MRS. DANVERS comes across and opens a second set of curtains, letting in a great deal of light.

MRS. DANVERS

A lovely room, isn't it? The loveliest room you've ever seen. Everything is kept just as Mrs. de Winter liked it. Nothing has been altered since that last night.

The girl automatically follows MRS. DANVERS as she passes to a small anteroom.

SEMI CLOSE UP

In a small anteroom lined with cupboards MRS. DANVERS suddenly stops. She indicates the cupboards to "I."

MRS. DANVERS

Come, I'll show you her dressing room. This is where I keep all her clothes. You would like to see them, wouldn't you?

"I" nods. As MRS. DANVERS opens the door of one closet, we see it is lined with furs. MRS. DANVERS takes out a chinchilla. She holds it out to "I".

MRS. DANVERS

Feel this. It was a Christmas present from Mr. de
Winter. He was always giving her expensive gifts, the
whole year round.

CLOSE UP

"I" cannot take her eyes from MRS. DANVERS' face as the
chinchilla is held against her cheek.

SEMI CLOSE UP

MRS. DANVERS withdraws it and replaces it among the other
furs as she continues:

MRS. DANVERS (opening another wardrobe)

I keep her underwear on this side. Here are her under-
clothes in this drawer. They were made specially for
her by the nuns in the Convent of St. Claire.

I always used to wait up for her, no matter how late.
Sometimes she and Mr. de Winter didn't come home
until dawn. While she was undressing she'd tell me
about the party she'd been to . . . She knew everyone
that mattered—everyone loved her!

When she had finished her bath, she'd go into the
bedroom and go over to the dressing table.

She turns and goes towards it—"I" following obediently.

SEMI CLOSE UP

By the dressing table, MRS. DANVERS puts her hands on "I's"
shoulders and gently pilots her onto the stool.

MRS. DANVERS (suddenly)

Oh, you've moved her brush, haven't you?

(she carefully straightens the brushes)

There, that's better, just as she always laid it down. "Come on, Danny, hair drill," she would say. And I'd stand behind her like this . . .

(she moves behind, taking up a brush)

. . . and brush away for twenty minutes at a time. And then she would say, "Goodnight, Danny" and step into her bed.

MRS. DANVERS raises "I" from the stool and leads her towards the bed.

SEMI CLOSE UP

She leads her right to the bedside and up the two steps. "I's" breathing becomes heavier and heavier as she nears the breaking point.

MRS. DANVERS lifts up the monogramed nightdress case and carefully takes from it a black chiffon nightdress.

MRS. DANVERS

I embroidered this case for her myself, and I keep it here always.

MRS. DANVERS puts a hand inside the chiffon and spreads open her fingers.

MRS. DANVERS

Did you ever see anything so delicate? Look, you can see my hand through it.

Suddenly "I" breaks away and stumbles blindly towards the door. MRS. DANVERS follows her quietly.

SEMI CLOSE UP

At the door, MRS. DANVERS come a alongside her—saying in a low voice:

MRS. DANVERS

You wouldn't think she had been gone so long, would you? Sometimes when I walk along the corridor, I fancy I hear her just behind me—that quick, light step, I couldn't mistake it anywhere. It's not only in this room—it's in all the rooms in the house. I can almost hear it now.

(she is pleased by the effect of her words on "I")

Do *you* believe the dead come back and watch the living?

"I" *(too vehemently)*

NO! NO! I *don't* believe it!

MRS. DANVERS *(whispers)*

Sometimes I wonder if she doesn't come back here to Manderley and watch you and Mr. de Winter together. You look tired. Why don't you stay here a while and rest? . . . Listen to the sea . . .

"I" looks wildly about the room.

MRS. DANVERS

It's so soothing . . . Listen to it . . . listen . . . Listen to the sea.

We hear the boom of the distant surf—it grows louder and louder.

FADE OUT.

(There is a fire in the fireplace)

CLOSE UP on the monogram on Rebecca's address book, which fills the screen. CAMERA MOVES UP to show "I" staring at it. She has an expression of wild, hysterical despair. Suddenly she turns, looks all about the room, then back at the desk. She turns the book over so that the monogram is hidden. "I's" hand seizes the phone and lifts the receiver.

"I" *(into phone)*
Tell Mrs. Danvers I wish to see her immediately!

"I" hangs up the phone, yanks the drawer open, and start pulling out Rebecca's lists and papers. A folded card is revealed at the bottom of the drawer. It is an engraved invitation card that says:

Mr. and Mrs. Maximilian de Winter
request the pleasure of Mr. Jack Favell's
presence at a costume ball
at Manderley
Thursday, June the fifteenth
Ten o'clock

and on it is scrawled:

Rebecca—
I'll be there—and how!
Jack

MRS. DANVERS enters.

MRS. DANVERS
You sent for me, Madam?

"I" looks up as MRS. DANVERS comes in. Her face is grimly set, as though she were ready for a fight.

"I"

Yes, Mrs. Danvers. I want you to get rid of all these things.

MRS. DANVERS looks down toward the desk.

MRS. DANVERS

These are Mrs. de Winter's things.

"I" *(with quiet determination)*

I am Mrs. de Winter now.

MRS. DANVERS *(with a slight bow)*

Very well. I will give the instructions.

The sound of an automobile horn is heard. "I" turns eagerly toward the window. MRS. DANVERS is just about to exit into the hall.

"I's" voice *(coldly)*

Just a moment, please.

MRS. DANVERS stops and turns.

CLOSE TWO SHOT

"I"

Mrs. Danvers, I intend to say nothing to Mr. de Winter about Mr. Favell's visit. In fact, I prefer to forget *everything* that happened this afternoon.

She goes out past MRS. DANVERS, who looks after her grimly.

INT. HALL—LONG SHOT—DUSK

MAXIM comes into the hall from the front door. "I" runs to him, throws her arms about him, and holds him frantically.

"I" *(in his arms)*
Oh, Maxim, Maxim! You've been gone all day.

MAXIM *(laughs)*
I'm choking! Well, well! What have you been doing with yourself?

"I"
I've been thinking.

MAXIM *(smiling)*
What did you want to do that for?

"I"
Come into the library, and I'll tell you.

They walk together into the library.

INT. LIBRARY

"I"
Darling, could we have a costume ball—just as you used to?

MAXIM *(surprised)*
Now what put that into your mind? Has Beatrice been at you?

"I"

No! I just feel we ought to *do* something—to make people feel that Manderley is the just the same as it always was. Please, darling, could we?

MAXIM *(trying gently to put her off)*

You don't know what it would mean, you know. You'd have to be hostess to hundreds of people—all the county—and a lot of young people would come up from London and turn this house into a nightclub.

"I" *(pleading)*

Yes, but I want to, MAXIM. Please. I've never been to a large party—but I can learn what to do. I *promise* you, you wouldn't be ashamed of me.

He looks into her eyes. Her face is so eager, so appealing that he relaxes and takes her in his arms.

MAXIM *(tolerantly)*

All right—if you think you'd enjoy it. You'd better get Mrs. Danvers to help you, hadn't you.

"I"

No, no, I don't need Mrs. Danvers to help me. I can do it myself.

MAXIM

All right, my sweet.

(kisses her)

"I" *(while she is being kissed)*

Oh, thank you, darling. Thank you. What will you go as?

MAXIM (*smiling at her*)

I never dress up. That's the one privilege I claim as the host. And what will you be? Alice in Wonderland—with that ribbon round your hair?

"I" (*happily*)

No, I won't tell you. I'll design my own costume and give you the surprise of your life!

CLOSE UP—SKETCH BOOK.

"I" is sketching in her bedroom. "I's" hand is adding a few strokes to a design for a costume. It is a female suit of armor, like that of Joan of Arc. She scratches it out, throws it on to a pile of other rejected sketches, and continues on to another. A knock at the door.

"I" (*preoccupied*)

Come in.

MRS. DANVERS enters, holding a few slightly crumpled sketches in her hand.

MRS. DANVERS

Robert found those sketches in the library, Madam. Did you intend throwing them away?

"I"

Yes, Mrs. Danvers, I did. They were just some ideas I was sketching for my costume for the ball.

MRS. DANVERS

Hasn't Mr. de Winter suggested anything?

"I" *(hesitantly)*

No. I want to surprise him. I don't want him to know anything about it.

MRS. DANVERS

I merely thought that you might find a costume among the family portraits that would suit you . . .

"I" *(rising)*

Do you mean those at the top of the stairs? I'll go and look at them.

She goes out into the hall, followed by MRS. DANVERS.

MOVING SHOT—GALLERY—DAY

"I" and Mrs. MRS. DANVERS walk along the gallery, looking up at the departed de Winters.

MRS. DANVERS

This one, for instance.

She turns and indicates the portrait of Caroline de Winter behind them.

MRS. DANVERS

It might have been designed for you, I'm sure you could have it copied.
Anxious to be convinced, "I" looks back at Mrs. Danvers and then to the picture again, uncertainly.

MRS. DANVERS

I've heard Mr. de Winter say this is his favorite of all the paintings. It's Lady Caroline de Winter, one of his ancestors.

"I" remains gazing at the picture as MRS. DANVERS, after a slight pause, moves silently away. "I," with almost a touch of relief combined with delight, turns spontaneously.

"I"

That's a splendid idea, Mrs. Danvers . . . I'm very grateful.

FADE OUT.

FADE IN:
INT. HALL—SEMI LONG SHOT—
NIGHT

It is a dark and foggy night. In the hall in Manderley is a long table garlanded and decorated with candles for the ball. On it is set the usual type of buffet supper, served for such an affair. Behind the table stand a couple of men servants and half a dozen maids ready to wait on the guests, when they arrive. FRITH is superintending last final touches to the preparations. FRANK CRAWLEY enters dressed in a mortar board and B.A. gown.

FRANK

Everything under control, Frith?

FRITH

Yes, sir, thank you.

(pause)

Excuse me, sir, are you supposed to be a schoolmaster?

FRANK

Not exactly—just my old cap and gown.

· 107 ·

FRITH

It certainly makes a very nice costume, sir—and economical too.

FRANK

Yes, that was the idea.

MED. SHOT—INT. LOBBY OF HALL

In the lobby, MAXIM descends the stairs to greet his guests. As ROBERT opens the door, we can see the fog outside. GILES and BEATRICE enter, GILES wearing bowler hat and overcoat, and BEATRICE in a long coat with a handkerchief tied over her headdress.

> **GILES** (*as he divests himself of his coat*)
> Evening, Robert. Not very good weather for the ball. Very misty on the way. Very chilly.

By this time GILES' coat is off, revealing him dressed in faded white tights with long sleeves and a high neck—over the tights is an imitation tiger skin. Long blonde braids hang down BEATRICE'S back.

BEATRICE

Wig's so blasted tight—they ought to have sent an aspirin with it.

By this time MAXIM has joined the two at the door; he surveys them both.

MAXIM

What's the idea? Adam and Eve?

BEATRICE

Oh, MAXIM, don't be disgusting.

GILES

Strong man, old man. Where's my weight thing?

BEATRICE

You didn't leave it in the car, did you?

At this moment their chauffeur appears, carrying a large pair of imitation spherical weights, joined by a painted wooden bar. The way he holds it shows that it has no weight at all. He hands them to GILES.

GILES

Oh, there it is.

BEATRICE

Are you the only one down? Where's the child?

MAXIM

She's keeping her costume a terrific secret, wouldn't even let me into her room.

BEATRICE

Lovely. I'll go up and give her a hand.

She exits. GILES and MAXIM go to join FRANK in the hall.

GILES

I could do with a drink.

MAXIM *(indicating Giles' costume)*

Won't you catch cold, in that thing?

GILES

Don't be silly. (Fingering his tights). Pure wool, old boy.

ROBERT enters the picture carrying the weights.

ROBERT

Pardon me, sir, you forgot this.

ROBERT drops the weights. They are inflated, so they bounce. GILES picks them up with an indignant glance at ROBERT.

INT. CORRIDOR—
SEMI CLOSE UP—NIGHT

Outside the door of "I's" room, BEATRICE is knocking. She starts to turn the handle.

BEATRICE

Here I am dear—it's Bee. I've come to give you a hand.

"I" (calling from inside)

Please don't come in, Beatrice. I don't want anyone to see my costume.

BEATRICE

Oh, well, you won't be long, will you? Because the first people will be arriving any moment.

She moves away from the door.

INT. "I'S" BEDROOM—
SEMI CLOSE UP

CLARICE, a very young maid, is kneeling on the ground putting finishing touches to the wide skirt of "I's" fancy dress.

"I"

Now you're sure that's where it should be?

CLARICE

Yes, Madam, just right. Oh, *yes*, Madam. It's *just* right.

"I" is dressed in a copy of the striking costume in the painting of Caroline de Winter. She is admiring herself in the mirror, turning her shoulders this way and that.

> **"I"**
>
> Isn't it exciting!

> **CLARICE**
>
> Indeed it is, Madam. I've always heard about the Manderley ball—and now I'm really going to see one. I'm sure there will be no one there to touch you, Madam!

> **"I"**
>
> Oh, do you really think so? . . . Where's my fan?

While CLARICE fetches the fan, "I" has a last, loving look at herself, then she takes the fan.

> **"I"**
>
> You're sure I look all right?

> **CLARICE** *(reverently)*
>
> You look ever so beautiful.

> **"I"**
>
> Well, here goes!

She starts towards the door; CLARICE darts ahead of her to open it.

> *INT. CORRIDOR—*
> *SEMI CLOSE UP—NIGHT*

The door of "I's" room opens and "I" emerges. As she comes along the corridor, she pats her hair, and fusses with parts of her dress. Her pace increases until she comes opposite the picture. She pulls up for a moment to compare herself with the original. Almost preening herself, she adopts the pose of the picture and, changing her pace to a dignified one, starts to move away towards the staircase.

With a light step, she starts to descend the stairs. When she reaches the bottom, she pauses, catches her breath, and starts to move forward towards them across the floor. MAXIM's back is turned toward her.

"I"

Good evening, Mr. de Winter.

MAXIM turns—still laughing and changing to a smile of anticipation on hearing her voice. Slowly the smile begins to fade from his face, and he eyes her up and down. A look of deep anger takes its place. "I's" expression changes from the excited smile to one of crushed bewilderment.

MAXIM takes half a step towards her—and speaks fiercely.

MAXIM

What the devil do you think you're doing?

"I" almost backs away from him. We see the startled faces of FRANK and GILES. BEATRICE is the last one to see her.

BEATRICE's hand flies to her mouth as though she would suppress her own cry of:

BEATRICE

Rebec . . . O . . . Oh . . . no . . .

"I," gazing with petrified eyes at MAXIM, gestures weakly:

"I"

It's—it's the picture — the one in the gallery.

MAXIM does not reply—he stands facing her like stone.

"I" *(desperately)*

What is it? What have I done?

MAXIM takes one step towards her and speaks in an icy tone.

MAXIM

Go and take it off! It doesn't matter what else you put
on . . . anything will do.

"I" stands motionless—unable to believe what she has heard
MAXIM say.

MAXIM

What are you standing there for—didn't you hear
what I said?

"I" looks about her desperately—then suddenly she turns and
dashes towards the stairs. MAXIM takes a step forward as if
he might follow her, but at this moment ROBERT announces
in a loud voice:

ROBERT

Sir George and Lady Moore.

(and then)

Mr. Dudley Tennant—

(again)

Admiral and Lady Burbank.

The first guests are arriving—a flock of about eight. We hear
their laughing chatter. MAXIM is forced to turn and play the
part of host.

"I" rushes along the corridor until she comes to the picture—then pulls up suddenly. She looks at it, then turning her
head towards the west wing, she sees MRS. DANVERS standing

there, a smile of supreme triumph on her face. MRS. DANVERS turns and goes through the door. "I" runs after her.

"I" nearly reaches the door of Rebecca's room—it is just closing. She hurries to it and then, bracing herself with courage, pushes the door open and goes in.

MRS. DANVERS

I watched you go down—just as I watched her a year ago. Even in the same dress you couldn't compare.
"I" takes a step nearer to her—she looks down at the dress, then back to MRS. DANVERS.

"I"

You knew it? You knew she wore it and yet you deliberately suggested that *I* wear it!

"I" leans toward MRS. DANVERS.

"I" *(with great intensity)*
Why do you hate me? What have I ever done to you that you should hate me so?

MRS. DANVERS *(speaking into the mirror)*
You tried to take her place. You let him marry you. I've seen his face, his eyes—they're the same as those first weeks after she died, when he shut himself up in his room. I used to listen to him—walking up and down, up and down, all night long, night after night. Thinking of her—suffering torture, because he'd lost her.

"I"

I don't want to know—I don't want to know.

MRS. DANVERS

You thought you could be Mrs. de Winter—live in her house—walk in her steps—take the things that were hers. But she's too strong for you. *You* can't fight her. No one ever got the better of her—never, never. She was beaten in the end. But it wasn't a man—it wasn't a woman—it was the sea!

"I" *(unable to bear any more)*
Stop, stop, I tell you . . .

She throws herself on the bed, breaking into convulsive sobs.

MRS. DANVERS stands looking down at the sobbing figure. A new thought comes into her face.

MRS. DANVERS comes to the window and throws it open. We see a heavy mist outside—there is a slight movement of the curtains. She glances round toward the window. Then turning back again to the bed, she speaks with uncanny calmness.

MRS. DANVERS

You're overwrought, Madam. I've opened a window for you. A little air will do you good.

"I" raises herself from her lying position and moves across toward the window, gasping for breath.

MRS. DANVERS

Why don't you go? . . . Why don't you leave Manderley? He doesn't need you. He's got his memories. He doesn't love you—he wants to be alone again with *her.*

"I's" face looks down to the depths below.

MRS. DANVERS

You've nothing to stay for. You've nothing to live for,
really, have you? Look down there. It's easy, isn't it?
Why don't you? . . .

"I" stares out, hypnotized, then slowly looks down again. In
her eyes we see the growing thought of self-destruction.

MRS. DANVERS

Why don't you? . . . Go on . . . go on . . . Don't be
afraid . . .

Suddenly the silence and the mist are shattered by an explo-
sion. Then another, accented by the strident wailing of a siren;
then a third. "I" stands frightened and mystified. From below
comes the sound of doors being opened. MRS. DANVERS,
with regained control, steps back.

Outside, the running figures of the guests emerging from
the front and side doors of the house. They are hardly discern-
ible in the mist, but we hear their voices.

MAN'S VOICE

Ship on the rocks!

ANOTHER MAN'S VOICE

Shipwreck!

THIRD MAN'S VOICE

Notify the Coast Guard! She's aground!

MAXIM

Come on, everybody—down to the bay—ship ashore!

"I" hears MAXIM's voice. She cries down to him.

"I"

Maxim! Maxim!

SEMI LONG SHOT

Below, MAXIM half turns as though he heard something. He hesitates for a moment, then runs on, his figure disappearing into the mist. "I" glares at MRS. DANVERS as she leaves the room. MRS. DANVERS turns aside, looking confused and distraught.

FADE IN:
EXT. COVE—DAWN—LONG SHOT

In the dim half-light of dawn with shafts of sunlight just beginning to penetrate the blanket of fog, we can vaguely discern the outline of rocks. We hear the pounding of the surf and the scream of gulls. In the distance we hear the shouts of the men who are helping to raise the boat: "They'll never shift 'er, not with that tide." "Diver's gone down again." "Headed for the reef—runs out quite a way." "Lend a hand here." Vague figures, clad for the most part in oilskins, loom out of the mist and go towards the direction of the shouts.

"I" appears scrambling down over the rocks.

Suddenly "I" gives a little scream. In the half light she has stumbled against a figure crouched down beside the breakwater. It is BEN. He scrambles to his feet.

TWO SHOT—BEN AND "I"

"I" *(smiling kindly at him)*
Ben, have you seen Mr. de Winter anywhere?

BEN stares at her foolishly, shaking his head—then, suddenly becoming slightly hysterical:

BEN

She won't come back no more, will she? You said so.

"I"

Who, Ben? What do you mean?

BEN (*jerking his thumb towards the sea*)
Her. The other one.

"I," realizing she can get nothing out of BEN as to the where-abouts of MAXIM, passes on.

FRANK comes up, bareheaded, and wearing a mackintosh. "I" seizes FRANK's arm.

"I"

Frank, have you seen Maxim anywhere?

FRANK

Not since about half an hour ago. I thought he'd gone up to the house.

"I"

No, he hasn't been home at all, and I'm afraid something might have happened to him.

There is a moment's silence as "I" looks curiously at FRANK, and he shifts a little uncomfortably under her gaze.

"I"

Frank, what's the matter? Is anything wrong? There *is* something wrong.

FRANK

When the diver went down to inspect the bottom of the ship, he found the hull of another boat—a little sailboat . . .

"I"

Frank, is it . . .?

FRANK *(looking her in the eyes)*

Yes . . . it was Rebecca's.

"I" digests this in silence for a moment, then speaks quietly:

"I"

How did they recognize it?

FRANK

He's a local man; he knew it instantly.

"I"

Oh, that's going to be so hard on poor Maxim . . .

FRANK

Yes. It'll bring it all back again, and worse than before.

"I"

Why did they have to find it? Why couldn't they have left it there in peace—at the bottom of the sea?

FRANK *(after a moment, embarrassed)*

I'd better get along and arrange some breakfast for the men.

"I"

All right, Frank, I'll go look for Maxim.

FRANK goes off. "I" stands indecisively for a second. We can still hear shouts from the men helping to raise the boat, and the noise of the waves. She starts to walk hesitantly in the direction from which the shouts come.

· **119** ·

As "I" scrambles over the rocks and into the cove, she looks across to the cottage.

Suddenly her attention is arrested as she sees a lamp alight in the window of the cottage, and firelight throwing flickering shadows on the windowpane. Determinedly but nervously she hurries toward the cottage and opens the door.

Inside the cottage, she is confronted by the figure of MAXIM, sitting in a corner.

"I" *(in amazement)*

MAXIM!

MAXIM *(turning)*

Hello—

"I" advances toward him, extremely worried. MAXIM has a disheveled look, but it is more than that: he has the air of a man who has come to the end of his tether.

"I" *(as she gets near him)*

MAXIM—you haven't had any sleep. Have you forgiven me?

MAXIM

Forgiven you? What have I got to forgive you for?

"I"

For last night—my stupidity about the costume.

MAXIM

Oh, that! . . . I'd forgotten. I was angry with you, wasn't I?

"I" *(shyly)*

Mm.

*(There is a moment's silence.
She looks at him pleadingly)*

MAXIM, can't we start all over again? I don't ask that you should love me . . . I won't ask impossible things. I'll be your friend, your companion . . . I'll be happy with that.

He looks at her strangely, takes her face between his hands and looks at her, tortured.

MAXIM

You love me very much, don't you? But it's too late, my darling . . . We've lost our little chance of heaven.

"I" *(frantically)*

No, Maxim, no!

MAXIM

Yes. It's all over now. The thing's happened—the thing I've dreaded day after day, night after night.

"I"

Maxim, what are you trying to tell me?

MAXIM

Rebecca has won.

"I" looks at him, her worst fears realized: he still loves Rebecca. After a moment, he speaks again.

MAXIM

Her shadow has been between us all the time—keeping us from one another. She knew that this would happen.

"I" *(gazing at him, speaking in stifled voice)*
What are you saying?

MAXIM

They sent a diver down. He found another boat—

"I" *(interrupting, comfortingly,*
but somewhat relieved)
Yes, I know. Frank told me. Rebecca's boat. It's terrible
for you,
    I'm so sorry.

MAXIM

The diver made another discovery. He broke one of the
ports and looked into the cabin. There was a body in
there.

"I" reacts sharply to this, bewildered at the tone of utter fatality with which MAXIM speaks.

"I"

Then she wasn't alone. There was someone sailing
with her and you have to find out who it was. That's it,
isn't it, Maxim?

MAXIM

You don't understand. There was no one with her.
(a moment's pause while she looks at him)
It's Rebecca's body lying there on the cabin floor.

"I"

No, no!

MAXIM

The woman that was washed up at Edgecoombe—the woman that is now embedded in the family crypt—that wasn't Rebecca. It was the body of some unknown woman, unclaimed, belonging nowhere. I identified it, but I knew it wasn't Rebecca. It was all a lie. *I* knew where Rebecca's body was! Lying on that cabin floor, on the bottom of the sea.

"I" *(terrified)*

How did you know, Maxim?

MAXIM

Because—I put it there!

Will you look into my eyes and tell me that you love me now?

MAXIM is searching her eyes. He reads there that she is stunned, overwhelmed, horrified by what he has told her. She turns and walks away from him.

MAXIM

You see, I was right. It's too late.

"I" comes into scene toward MAXIM, her heart jumping in quickened, sudden panic.

"I"

No, it's not too late!

(she puts her arms around him)

You're not to say that! I love you more than anything in the world . . . Please, Maxim, kiss me, please!

MAXIM

No. It's no use. It's too late.

"I"

We can't lose each other now! We've got to be together—always! With no secrets, no shadows . . .

MAXIM

We may only have a few days, a few hours.

"I" (pleadingly)

Oh, Maxim, why didn't you tell me before?

MAXIM

I nearly did several times, but somehow you never seemed close enough.

"I" (looks at him)

How could we be close when I know you were always thinking of Rebecca? How could I even ask you to love me when I knew you loved Rebecca still?

MAXIM

What are you talking about? What do you mean?

"I"

Whenever you touched me, I knew you were comparing me with Rebecca. Whenever you spoke to me or looked at me, walked with me in the garden, I knew you were thinking, "This I did with Rebecca—and this, and this . . ."

MAXIM stares at her, bewildered, amazed, then turns slightly away.

"I" (takes a step toward him)

It's true, isn't it?

MAXIM *(whips around)*

You thought I loved Rebecca? You thought that? I *hated* her!

"I" is incredulous. MAXIM starts to pace up and down, speaking in an almost quiet, reflective voice.

MAXIM

Oh, I was carried away by her, enchanted by her, as everyone was. And when I was married, I was told I was the luckiest man in the world . . . she was so lovely, so accomplished, so amusing. "She's got the three things that really matter in a wife," everyone told me, "Breeding, brains, and beauty". . . and I believed her—completely . . . But I never had a moment's happiness with her . . . She was incapable of love, or tenderness, or decency.

There is exultation in "I"'s face as she looks at him.

"I" *(almost to herself)*

You didn't love her! You didn't love her!

MAXIM

Do you remember that cliff where you first saw me in Monte Carlo? Well—I when there with Rebecca on our honeymoon . . . That's when I found out about her—four days after we were married . . . She stood there laughing, her black hair blowing in the wind. She told me all about herself—everything . . . things I'll never tell a living soul.

MAXIM moves off abruptly.

MAXIM

I wanted to kill her. It would have been so easy. You remember the precipice? I frightened you, didn't I? You thought I was mad. Perhaps I was. Perhaps I am mad. It wouldn't make for sanity, would it, living with the devil?

"I'll make a bargain with you," she told me. "You'd look rather foolish trying to divorce me now, after four days of marriage. So I'll play the part of a devoted wife, mistress of your precious Manderley. I'll make it the most famous showplace in England, if you like, and people will visit us and envy us and say we're the luckiest, happiest couple in the country. What a grand joke it will be! What a triumph!"

He comes to a halt and swings around to "I." She looks up at him with deep compassion, as he continues, in desperate self-accusation:

MAXIM

I should never have accepted her dirty bargain. But I did. I was younger then—and tremendously conscious of—(contemptuously) "the family honor." The family honor!

She knew I'd sacrifice everything rather than stand in a divorce court and give her away, admit that our marriage was a rotten fraud.

You despise me, don't you, as I despise myself? You can't understand what my feelings were, can you?

"I" *(with infinite tenderness)*
Of course I can, darling. Of course I can.

MAXIM

I kept the bargain—and so did she—apparently. Oh, she played the game brilliantly . . . But after a while she began to grow careless. She took a flat in London, and she'd stay away for days at a time . . . Then she started to bring her friends down here. I warned her, but she shrugged her shoulders. "What's it got to do with you?" she said . . . She even started on Frank, poor faithful Frank . . . Then there was a cousin of hers—a man named Favell.

"I"

I know him. He came here the day you went to London.

MAXIM

Why didn't you tell me?

"I"

I didn't like to. I thought it would remind you of—Rebecca.

MAXIM

Remind me!

(with a laugh)

As if I needed reminding! Favell used to visit her here— in this cottage. I found out about it and I warned her if I found him here again, I'd shoot them both.

One night, when I found she'd come back quietly from London, I thought Favell was with her. And I knew then that I couldn't stand this life of filth and deceit any longer. I decide to come down here and have it out with both of them. But she was alone. She was expecting Favell, but he hadn't come.

She was lying on the divan, a large tray of cigarette stubs beside her. She looked ill—queer. Suddenly she got up, started to walk toward me.

"When I have a child," she said, "neither you nor anyone else could ever prove it wasn't yours. You'd like an heir, wouldn't you, Max, for your beloved Manderley?" And she started to laugh. "How funny . . . how supremely, wonderfully funny! I'll be the perfect mother—just as I've been the perfect wife. No one will ever know. It ought to give you the thrill of your life, Max, to watch my son grow bigger day by day and to know that when you die—Manderley will be *his*!"

She was face to face with me, one hand in her pocket, the other holding a cigarette. She was smiling. "Well, Max, what are you going to do about it? Aren't you going to kill me?" I suppose I went mad for a moment . . . I must have struck her. She stood staring at me. She looked—almost triumphant. Then she started toward me again, laughing. Then suddenly she stumbled and fell. When I looked down—ages afterwards, it seemed—she was lying on the floor. She had struck her head on a heavy piece of ship's tackle. I remember wondering why she was still smiling . . . And then I realized she was dead.

"I"

But you didn't kill her . . . it was an accident!

MAXIM

Who would believe me? I lost my head . . . I just knew I had to do something—anything. I carried her out to the boat. It was very dark. There was no moon. I put her in the cabin. When the boat seemed a safe distance from the shore, I took a spike and drove it again and again through the planking of the hull. I'd opened up the seacocks and the water began to come in fast. I climbed into the dinghy and pulled away. I saw the boat keel over and sink . . . I pulled back to the cove . . . It started raining . . .

"I"

Does anyone else know this?

MAXIM *(shakes his head)*

No one—except you and me.

"I" becomes alert, intelligent, mature, taking command of the situation. She is the adult wife concerned with her husband's safety.

"I"

We must explain it. It's got to be the body of someone you've never seen before.

MAXIM

They're bound to know her . . . The bracelets and rings she always wore . . . They'll identify her body, and then they'll remember the other woman—the other woman buried in the crypt.

"I" *(clipping out orders)*

If they find out it's Rebecca, you must say simply that you made a mistake about the other body. You must say that when you went to Edgecoombe you were ill, you didn't know what you were doing. Rebecca's dead, that's what we've got to remember! Rebecca's dead. She can't speak—she can't bear witness. She can't harm you anymore. We're the only two people in the world who will ever know, MAXIM—you and I.

MAXIM

I told you once that I'd done a very selfish thing in marrying you. You can understand now what I meant. I've loved you, my darling—I shall always love you—but I've known all along that Rebecca would win in the end!

"I"

No! No! She *hasn't* won! No matter what happens now—she *hasn't* won!

They cling to each other desperately. They are really together for the first time with no secret between them.

Suddenly the phone rings jarringly. MAXIM picks up the phone.

MAXIM *(into phone)*

Hello . . .

(pause)

Hello, Frank . . . Who? Colonel Julyan! (pause) Yes, tell him I'll meet him there as soon as I possibly can. What? Well, say we can talk about that when we're sure about the matter.

He hangs up.

"I"

What's happened?

MAXIM

Colonel Julyan called . . . He's the chief constable of the county. He's been asked by the police to go to the mortuary. He wants to know if I could possibly have made a mistake about—that other body.

The two of them stand looking at each other, the girl terrified as to what this may mean. MAXIM steps toward her, puts his arms around her.

FADE OUT.

DISSOLVE IN:
MED. SHOT—DAY

Five men, two of them policemen in uniform, are in an interrogation room: MAXIM, COLONEL JULYAN, and FRANK are the others. MAXIM is in the middle of the group, but we can see no faces. After a moment, MAXIM turns slightly and nods to the man on his left. Then he turns completely and walks away from the group, COLONEL JULYAN and FRANK following him.

MAXIM

Well, Colonel Julyan, apparently I did make a mistake about that other body.

FRANK

The mistake was quite natural under the circumstances. Besides, you weren't well at the time.

MAXIM

That's nonsense—I was perfectly well.

JULYAN

Don't let it worry you, Maxim. Nobody can blame you for making a mistake. Pity is, you've got to go through the same thing all over again.

MAXIM

What do you mean?

JULYAN

Well, there'll have to be another inquest, of course. Same formality and red tape. Wish you could be spared the publicity of it, but I'm afraid that's impossible.

MAXIM

Oh yes—the publicity.

JULYAN

I suppose that Mrs. de Winter went below for something, and the squall hit the boat when there was no body at the helm. I imagine that's the solution, don't you, Crawley?

FRANK

Oh, yes. Probably the door jammed, and she couldn't get up on deck again.

JULYAN

Tabb will undoubtedly come to some type of conclusion.

FRANK

Why? What would he know about it?

JULYAN

Well, he's examining the boat now. Purely a matter of routine, you know. I'll be at the inquest tomorrow, Maxim, quite unofficially, you know. We must get together for a game of golf when it's all over, eh? Bye-bye.

FADE OUT.

FADE IN:
LONG SHOT—HALL AT
MANDERLEY—NIGHT

We see "I" come down the stairs of the Manderley hall. She is simply attired. FRITH is approaching from another direction, two or three newspapers in his hand.

FRITH

I have the evening papers, madam. Would you care to see them?

"I"

No, thank you, Frith, and I'd prefer that Mr. de Winter were not troubled with them either.

FRITH

I understand, Madam . . . Permit me to say that we're all most distressed outside.

"I"

Thank you, Frith.

FRITH

I'm afraid the news has been a great shock to Mrs. Danvers.

"I"

Yes, I rather expected it would be.

FRITH *(hesitantly)*

It seems there's to be a coroner's inquest, Madam?

"I"

Yes, Frith, it's purely a formality.

FRITH

Of course, madam. I wanted to say that if any of us
might be required to give evidence, I should be only
too pleased to do anything that might help the family.

"I" *(touched)*

Thank you, Frith. I'm sure Mr. de Winter will be very
happy to hear it. But I don't think anything will be
necessary.

**She gives him a kindly look and walks off as he bows slightly.
"I" strolls into the library.**

LIBRARY—(FIRE GOING?)

**In the library, MAXIM is standing at the fireplace, his back to
the door, smoking moodily. He turns as the girl comes in and
affects cheeriness.**

"I"

Max.

MAXIM *(tenderly)*

Hello, darling.

"I"

Oh, Maxim, I'm worried about what you'll do at the
inquest tomorrow.

MAXIM

What do you mean?

"I"

You won't lose your temper, will you? Promise you
won't let them make you angry.

MAXIM *(after a moment)*

All right, darling . . . I promise.

"I"

No matter what he asks you, you won't lose your head?

MAXIM

Don't worry, dear.

"I"

They can't do anything at once, can they?

MAXIM

No.

"I"

Then we've a little time left to be together?

MAXIM

Yes.

"I"

I want to go to the inquest with you.

MAXIM

I'd rather you didn't, darling.

"I"

But I can't wait here alone . . . I promise you I won't be any trouble to you . . . I must be near you so that no matter what happens we won't be separated for a moment.

MAXIM

All right. I don't mind this whole thing—except for you. I can't forget what it's done. I've been thinking of nothing also since it happened. . . . (He lifts her chin and looks her in the face.) It's gone forever . . . that funny, young, lost look that I loved. It won't ever come back again. I killed that when I told you about Rebecca. It's gone . . . in a few hours . . . You've grown so much older.

"I"

Maxim . . . Maxim . . .

He takes her in his arms and crushes her to him, and they kiss feverishly, desperately, like guilty lovers who have not kissed before and may never kiss again.

FADE IN:
EXT. CORONER'S COURT—DAY

A POLICEMAN is standing in front of the coroner's court, addressing a crowd.

POLICEMAN

Blackjack Bridey was his name. The most important arrest I ever made. It must have been about two years ago now. Course there was no doubt about it. He was 'ung a month after I caught him.
Now wait a minute.

The POLICEMAN opens the courtroom door.

They've got old balmy Ben up now.

BEN is standing in the courtroom as he is being questioned by the CORONER.

• **136** •

CORONER

You remember the late Mrs. de Winter, don't you?

BEN

She's gone.

CORONER *(slightly impatient)*

Yes—we know that.

BEN

She went into the sea. The sea got her.

CORONER

That's right. Now—we want you to tell us whether you were at the shore that last night when she went out and didn't come back?

Were you on the shore that last night, when she went out?

When she didn't come back?

BEN

I didn't see nothing. I don't want to go to the asylum! They'm cruel folks there.

CORONER

Now, now—nobody's going to send you to the asylum. All we want you to do is tell us what you saw.

BEN

I didn't see nothing!

CORONER

Come, come. Did you see Mrs. de Winter get into her boat that night?

BEN

I don't know nothing! I don't want to go to the asylum!

CORONER

Very well. You may go.

BEN

Eh?

CORONER

You may go now.

FAVELL, in the court, exchanges looks with MRS. DANVERS.

CORONER

Mr. Tabb, will you come forward?

TABB advances and stands holding the back of the witness chair. He is sworn in by the bailiff.

CORONER

The late Mrs. de Winter used to send her boat to your shipyard for reconditioning?

TABB

That's right, sir.

CORONER

Can you remember any occasion when she had any sort of an accident with the boat?

TABB

No, sir. I often said Mrs. de Winter was a born sailor.

CORONER

When Mrs. de Winter went below, as is supposed, and a sudden gust of wind came down, that would be enough to capsize the boat, wouldn't it?

TABB

Excuse me, sir, but there's a little more to it than that.

CORONER

What do you mean, Mr. Tabb?

TABB

I mean, sir, the seacocks.

CORONER

What are the seacocks?

TABB

The seacocks are the valves to drain out the boat. They're always kept tight closed when you're afloat.

CORONER

Yes?

TABB

Yesterday when I examined the boat, I found that they'd been opened.

CORONER

What could have been the reason for that?

TABB

Just this, sir. That's what flooded the boat and sunk her.

CORONER (gravely)

Are you implying that boat never capsized at all?

TABB

I know it's a terrible thing to say, sir, but in my opinion she was scuttled. And there's them holes.

CORONER

What holes?

TABB

In her planking.

CORONER

What are you talking about?

TABB

Of course, that boat's been under water for over a year, and the tide's been knocking her against the ridge. But it seemed to me, them holes looked as if she'd made 'em from the *inside*.

MAXIM'S face is almost mask-like in his effort to retain an outward show of imperturbability. The hubbub of excitement from the crowd has grown louder.

CLOSE UP—FRANK

Looking from MAXIM to "I" with extreme concern.

CORONER

And you believe she must have done it deliberately.

TABB

Couldn't have been no accident. Not with her knowledge of boats.

• 140 •

The CORONER leans across to speak in a low tone to COLONEL JULYAN.

CORONER

You knew the former Mrs. de Winter well, I believe?

JULYAN

Oh, yes.

CORONER

Would you have believed her capable of suicide?

JULYAN

No, frankly, I would not. But you never can tell.

CORONER

You may stand down, Mr. Tabb. Mr. de Winter, please.

MAXIM has now reached the witness chair. CORONER turns to him.

CORONER

I'm sorry to drag you back for further questioning, Mr. de Winter. But you've heard the statement from Mr. Tabb. I wonder if you can help us in any way.

MAXIM

I'm afraid not.

CORONER

Can you think of any reason there should have been holes in the planking of the late Mrs. de Winter's boat?

MAXIM

Of course I can't think of any reason.

CORONER

Has anyone ever discussed these holes with you before?

MAXIM

Well, sir, since the boat has been at the bottom of the ocean, I scarcely think that likely.

CORONER

Mr. de Winter, I want you to believe that we all feel very deeply for you in this matter, but you must remember I don't conduct this enquiry for my own amusement.

MAXIM

That's rather obvious, isn't it?

CORONER

I hope it is. Well, since she went sailing alone, are we to believe that she drilled those holes herself?

MAXIM

You may believe what you like.

CORONER

Can you enlighten us as to why Mrs. de Winter would have wanted to end her own life?

MAXIM

I know of no reason whatever.

"I" seems to be losing control. She hears the voices murmuring, which, although loud, are unintelligible, until the CORONER's voice comes through:

CORONER

Mr. de Winter, however painful it may be, I have to ask you a very personal question: were relations between you and the late Mrs. de Winter perfectly happy? *Were the relations between you and the late Mrs. de Winter perfectly happy?*

MAXIM

I won't stand for it any longer, and you might know now!

"I" faints and falls to the floor. There is a slight commotion in the court. MAXIM leaves the witness stand and hastens across to where "I" has fallen to the floor. He helps her up with the aid of FRANK.

CORONER

We'll adjourn until after lunch. Mr. de Winter, I presume you'll be available for us then?

MAXIM nods.

MAXIM is now supporting "I." He has his arm around her shoulder.

MAXIM *(tenderly)*

I told you you should have had some breakfast. You're hungry—that's what's the matter with you.

"I" responds to his forced cheerfulness by smiling wanly at him.

DISSOLVE TO:
EXT. INN YARD—DAY

Outside the courtroom, the yard is beginning to fill up with people emerging from the schoolroom, which is on the opposite side to the inn. Most of them are making their way toward the bar and dining room. There are three or four cars parked. MAXIM emerges from the schoolroom with "I," who has recovered a little. At this moment a large Rolls-Royce turns into the yard. The CHAUFFEUR pulls up on seeing MAXIM.

CHAUFFEUR

Mr. Frith thought you might like to have some lunch from the house, and sent me with it.

MAXIM *(cheerfully)*

That's fine, Mullen.

(indicating)

Can you pull around the corner?

CHAUFFEUR

Yes, very good, sir.

He exits, and MAXIM and "I" start walking, MAXIM guiding her.

"I"

Awfully foolish of me . . . fainting like that.

MAXIM *(tenderly)*

Nonsense. If you hadn't fainted like that I'd have *really* lost my temper.

"I"

Darling, *please* be careful.

• 144 •

He gives her arm an affectionate, reassuring little squeeze, and they are at the car, where the CHAUFFEUR is holding the door open.

>   **MAXIM** *(as "I" gets in)*
> Darling, wait here a few moments, I'll see if I can find old Frank.

>   **"I"**
> Of course, darling. Don't worry about me. I'll be all right.

MAXIM has been opening the basket, and now pulls out a flask of brandy and hands it to her:

>   **MAXIM**
> Here, try a spot of this. It'll do you good.

She takes it, smiling wanly at him.

>   **MAXIM**
> Are you all right?

>   **"I"**
> Yes, of course, darling.

>   **MAXIM**
> I won't be long.

>   **"I"**
> Right you are.

He exits.

CLOSE UP OF "I"

(with the brandy, making a wry face)

She looks over and sees FAVELL, who is leaning into the open car window, smiling slyly at her.

FAVELL

Hello, and how does the bride find herself today? I say, marriage with Max is not exactly a bed of roses, is it?

"I"

I think you'd better go before Maxim gets back.

FAVELL

Jealous, is he? Well, I can't say I blame him. But *you* don't think I'm the big bad wolf, do you? I'm not, you know. I'm a perfectly ordinary, harmless bloke. And I think you're behaving splendidly over all this . . . perfectly splendidly. You know, you've grown up a bit since I last saw you last.

"I" does not answer.

FAVELL

Well, it's no wonder . . .

MAXIM enters scene. For a moment FAVELL does not see him. MAXIM is clearly in a rage at finding FAVELL here.

MAXIM

What do you want, Favell?

FAVELL *(coolly)*

Hullo, Max. Things are going pretty well for you, aren't they? Better than you ever expected. I was rather worried about you at first. That's why I came to the inquest.

• **146** •

MAXIM

I'm touched by your solicitude, but if you'll excuse me, I'd rather like to have my lunch.

FAVELL, nothing daunted, looks down at the lunch basket. He steps into the car.

FAVELL

Lunch? I say, what a jolly idea! Rather like a picnic, isn't it?

Without being asked he dips into the basket, FAVELL takes a leg of chicken and starts to gnaw at it.

You know, Max, I really feel I ought to talk things over with you.

MAXIM (sharply)

Talk what things over?

FAVELL

Well, those holes in the planking, for one thing—those holes that were drilled from the *inside*. (he gets a sudden thought, leans back to the driver) Oh, Mullen . . .

CHAUFFEUR

Yes, sir?

FAVELL

I say, would you like a good fellow get my car filled with petrol? It's almost empty.

CHAUFFEUR

Of course, sir.

FAVELL

Oh, and Mullen, close the door, will you?

CHAUFFEUR

Yes, sir.

The CHAUFFEUR closes the car door and exits.

FAVELL *(indicating his cigarette)*

Does this bother you?

FAVELL tosses his cigarette out the window.

FAVELL *(resuming his munching)*

You know, I've a strong feeling, old boy, that before the day is out, somebody's going to make use of that expressive though rather old-fashioned term, "foul play."

FAVELL picks up the brandy flask and a small glass. He pours himself some brandy.

FAVELL

Am I boring you with all this? No? Good.

(he sips the brandy)

You see, Max, I'm finding myself in rather an awkward position.

FAVELL pulls a folded note from his pocket.

You've only got to read this note to understand. It's from Rebecca, and what's more, she had the foresight to put a date it. She wrote it to me on the day she died. Incidentally, I was out at a party that night, so I didn't get the note until the next day.

MAXIM

And what makes you think the note would interest
me?

FAVELL

Oh, I'm not going to bother you with the contents now,
but I can assure you that it is not the note of a woman
who intends to drown herself that same night.

FAVELL finishes chewing on the chicken leg.

FAVELL

By the way, what do you do with old bones? Bury
them. However, for the time being . . . (he throws the
chicken bone out the window).

You know, Max, I'm getting awfully fed up with my
job as a motor car salesman. I don't know if you've
experienced the feeling of driving in an expensive car
that isn't your own, but it can be very, very exasper-
ating. You know what I mean—you want to own the
car yourself.

I've often wondered what it'd be like to retire to the
country—have a little place with a few acres of shoot-
ing. I've never figured out what it'd cost a year, but I'd
like to talk it about it with you, Max. I'd like to have
your advice on how to live comfortably without hard
work . . .

FRANK appears at the window of the car.

FRANK *(coldly)*

Hello, Favell.

(in a different tone)

Were you looking for me, Maxim?

MAXIM

Yes. Mr. Favell and I have a little business transaction
on hand.

I think it would be better if we conducted it over at
the inn.

They may have a private room there.

MAXIM and FAVELL leave the car.

FAVELL raises his hat to "I," looks at her provocatively.

FAVELL

See you later.

MAXIM suddenly leans back into the car and quietly and hastily says to FRANK:

MAXIM

Find Colonel Julyan. Tell him I want to see him
immediately.

(to FAVELL)

Come on, Favell. Let's go.

INT. INN—DAY

As MAXIM and FAVELL enter the inn, the buzz of conversation dies down when most of the customers see who enters.
MAXIM goes over to the PROPRIETOR.

MAXIM

Have you a private room, please?

PROPRIETOR

Of course, sir, there, sir.

He immediately bustles into activity and loads them through a small door into another room. MAXIM and FAVELL enter, as the PROPRIETOR stands, servile, bowing them in.

PROPRIETOR

I hope this will do, Mr. de Winter?

FAVELL

It's splendid, splendid—exactly like the Ritz.

PROPRIETOR

Any orders, gents?

FAVELL

Yes, you might bring me a large brandy and soda. How about you, Max? Have one on me. I feel I can afford to play host.

MAXIM

Thanks. I don't mind if I do.

FAVELL *(turns to proprietor)*

Make it two.

PROPRIETOR

Very good, sir.

He exits. At that point, JULYAN, FRANK, and "I" enter.

MAXIM

This is Colonel Julyan, Mr. Favell.

FAVELL

Oh I know Colonel Julyan. We're old friends, aren't we, Colonel?

JULYAN stares at Favell coldly, doesn't reply.

MAXIM

Since you're old friends, I assume you know that he is also head of the police here. I think he might be interested to hear your proposition. Go on, Jack. Tell him all about it.

FAVELL

I don't know what you mean. I merely said I hoped to give up selling motor cars and retire into the country.

MAXIM

Actually he offered to withhold some vital evidence from the inquest if I'd make it worth his while.

FAVELL, looking steadily at MAXIM, switches his eyes to JULYAN and speaks calmly:

FAVELL

I only want to see justice done. That boat builder's evidence suggested certain possible theories concerning Rebecca's death . . .

One of them, of course, is suicide. Now I've a little note here, which I consider puts that possibility quite out of court . . . Read it, Colonel.

JULYAN *(reading)*

"Jack darling—I have just seen the doctor and I'm going down to Manderley right away. I shall be at the cottage all this evening, and shall leave the door open for you. I have something terribly important to tell you. —Rebecca."

FAVELL

Now does that look like a note from a woman who had made up her mind to kill herself? And apart from that, Colonel, do you mean to tell me that if you wanted to commit suicide, you'd go to all the trouble of putting out to sea in a boat, and then take a hammer and chisel, and laboriously knock holes through the bottom of it? Come, Colonel—as an officer of the law, don't you feel that there are some slight grounds for *suspicion*?

JULYAN *(gravely)*

Of murder?

FAVELL *(interrupting casually)*

What else? You've known Max a long time, so you know he's the old-fashioned type who'd die to defend his honor—or who'd kill for it!

FRANK *(steps up hurriedly and furiously)*

It's blackmail—blackmail pure and simple.

JULYAN

Blackmail is not so pure, nor so simple. It can bring a lot of trouble to a great many people, and sometimes the blackmailer finds himself in jail at the end of it.

FAVELL

Oh, I see. You're going to hold de Winter's hand through this. Just because he's the big noise around here and he's actually permitted you to dine with him.

JULYAN

Be careful, Favell . . . You've brought an accusation of murder. Have you any witnesses?

FAVELL

I do have a witness. It's that fellow Ben. If that stupid coroner hadn't been as much of a snob as you are, he'd have seen that halfwit was hiding something.

JULYAN

And why should Ben do that?

FAVELL

Because we caught him once, Rebecca and I, peering at us through the cottage window. Rebecca threatened him with the asylum. *That's* why he was afraid to speak. But he was always hanging about; he must have seen this whole thing . . .

FRANK *(breaking in)*

It's ridiculous even listening to all of this!

FAVELL

You're like a little trades union, all of you, aren't you? And if my guess is right, there's a bit of malice in your soul toward me, isn't there, Crawley? Crawley didn't have much success with Rebecca. But he ought to have more luck this time. The bride will be grateful for your fraternal arm, Crawley, in a week or so—every time she faints, in fact . . .

Suddenly MAXIM moves forward and strikes FAVELL on the point of the jaw, stopping his words. FAVELL crumples and falls as we hear:

JULYAN

De Winter!

"I" *(screams)*

Maxim, please!

(goes to him)

FAVELL *(nursing his jaw, rises, smiling)*
That temper of yours will do you in yet, Max.

There is a knock on the door. The PROPRIETOR enters with the drinks, places them before them.

PROPRIETOR

Excuse me, gentlemen. Now is there anything else?

FAVELL

Yes. You might bring Mr. de Winter a sedative.

JULYAN *(shortly to the PROPRIETOR)*
No, no, nothing at all. Just leave us.

The PROPRIETOR looks strangely around and exits from the room, closing the door. FAVELL reaches for one of the two drinks and drinks it greedily.

JULYAN

And now, Favell, let's get this business over with. Since you have this whole thing worked out so carefully, perhaps you can provide us with a motive?

FAVELL

I knew you were going to bring that up, Colonel. I've read enough detective stories to know there must always be a motive. And if you will all excuse me for a moment, I'll supply that too.

MAXIM looks at "I," sees the great alarm in her face. He tries to give her a reassuring smile.

MAXIM

I wish you'd go home. I don't think you ought to stay
through all this.

"I" (*pleadingly*)

No, no. Please let me stay, Maxim.

FRANK

Surely, Colonel, you're not going to allow this man to—

Before he can go on, JULYAN puts up a restraining hand.

JULYAN

My opinion of Favell is no higher than yours, Crawley,
but in my official capacity, I have no alternative but to
pursue his accusation.

As he has been speaking, we have heard the door
opening.

FAVELL

I agree with you entirely, Colonel.

FAVELL is standing at the door in an attitude of mock gravity.

FAVELL

In a matter so serious as this we should make sure
of every point, explore every avenue, in fact, to coin a
phrase, leave no stone unturned.

FAVELL looks past the open door.

Ah, here she is . . . the missing link . . . the witness
who will help supply the motive!

As he is saying these words, MRS. DANVERS has stepped into
the room, and FAVELL closes the door behind her.

FAVELL

Colonel Julyan—Mrs. Danvers. I believe you know everyone else.

JULYAN

Won't you sit down?

FAVELL pulls out a chair, which MRS. DANVERS ignores.

FAVELL

No offense, Colonel, but I think if *I* put this to Danny she'll understand it more easily.

(he turns back to Mrs. Danvers)

Danny—who was Rebecca's doctor?

MRS. DANVERS *(coldly)*

Mr. de Winter always had Dr. McClean from the village.

FAVELL *(urgently)*

Now you heard . . . I said *Rebecca's* doctor—in London.

MRS. DANVERS

I don't know anything about that.

FAVELL

Don't give me that, Danny. You knew everything about Rebecca. You knew she was in love with me, didn't you? Surely you haven't forgotten the good times she and I used to have down at the cottage on the beach.

MRS. DANVERS

She had a right to amuse herself, didn't she? Love was a game with her, only a game. It made her laugh, I tell you. She used to sit on her bed and rock with laughter at the lot of you.

JULYAN

Can you think of any reason why Mrs. de Winter should have taken her own life?

MRS. DANVERS

No . . . No. I refuse to believe it. I knew everything about her, and I *won't* believe it.

FAVELL

There—you see? It's impossible. She knows that as well as I do.

Listen to me, Danny . . . we know that Rebecca went to a doctor in London on the last day of her life. Who was it?

MRS. DANVERS

I don't know!

FAVELL

I understand, Danny. You think we're asking you to reveal secrets of Rebecca's life. You're trying to defend her. That's what *I'm* doing. I'm trying to clear her name of the suspicion of suicide.

JULYAN *(steps forward)*

Mrs. Danvers, it has been suggested that Mrs. de Winter was deliberately murdered.

FAVELL

There you have it in a nutshell, Danny. But there's one more thing you'll want to know—the name of the murderer. It's a lovely name that rolls off the tongue so easily—George Fortescue Maximilian de Winter.

MRS. DANVERS displays a look of horror.

MRS. DANVERS

There was a doctor. Mrs. de Winter sometimes went to him privately. She used to go to him even before she was married.

FAVELL

We don't want reminiscences, Danny. What was his name?

MRS. DANVERS

Dr. Baker—165 Goldhawk Road—Shepherd's Bush . . .

FAVELL (*triumphantly*)

There you are, Colonel! There's where you'll find your motive! Go and question Dr. Baker! He'll tell you why Rebecca went to him—to confirm the fact that she was going to have a child—a sweet, curly-headed little child.

MRS. DANVERS

It isn't true! It isn't true! She would have told me!

FAVELL

She told Max about it—Max, who knew *he* wasn't the father! So, like the gentleman of the old school that he is, he killed her!

JULYAN

I'm afraid we shall have to question this Dr. Baker.

FAVELL

Hear! Hear! . . . But for safety's sake, I think I'd like to go along too.

JULYAN

Yes, unfortunately, I suppose you have the right to ask
that . . .

(He starts out)

I shall see the coroner and arrange for the inquest to
be postponed ponding further evidence.

FAVELL *(watching JULYAN exit)*

Aren't you rather afraid that the—uh—shall we say
the prisoner will bol<u>t</u>?

JULYAN

You have *my* word for it that he will not do that.

(he exits)

FAVELL

Toodle-oo, Max, old boy . . . Come along Danny . . .
Let's leave the unhappy couple to spend their last
minutes together alone . . .

He starts to leave—MRS. DANVERS following. She throws a
cold glance at MAXIM and exits.

DISSOLVE TO:
EXT. INN—DAY

Outside the inn is the big de Winter car. MAXIM is walking
with "I" toward the cars, FRANK behind them.

"I" *(concealing all emotion)*

Are you sure you don't want me to go with you, Max?

MAXIM

You'd better not, darling. The journey would be very tiring for you . . . I'll be back the very first thing in the morning. I won't even stop to sleep.

"I" *(simply, covering her*
own feelings completely)

I'll be waiting for you.

She kisses him and gets into the large car. The CHAUFFEUR steps into the scene. MAXIM gives him a nod to leave, which he does. MAXIM closes the door of the car himself, as JULYAN enters.

JULYAN

Ready, MAXIM?

MAXIM

Yes.

JULYAN

You two go along ahead. I'll follow along with Favell.

The road is either in the country or somewhere that looks like the suburbs of London. One car is following the other, both speeding.

DISSOLVE

FADE IN:
EXT. GOLDHAWK ROAD—
EXTREME LONG SHOT—
(STOCK)—NIGHT

Goldhawk Road, Shepherd's Bush. A house which has steps leading up to it, rather like a New York brownstone house, the cars of MAXIM and FAVELL are drawn up. MAXIM, JULYAN, CRAWLEY, and FAVELL are going up the steps.

DISSOLVE TO:
INT. CONSULTING ROOM—NIGHT

The four men and DR. BAKER are sitting in the doctor's consulting room.

JULYAN

Dr. Baker, you may have seen Mr. de Winter's name in the papers . . .

DR. BAKER

Oh yes . . . yes . . . In connection with the body that was found in a boat . . . My wife was reading all about it. Very sad case . . . My condolences, Mr. de Winter.

FAVELL

This is going to take hours—let me—

JULYAN *(interposes sharply)*

Don't bother, Favell . . . I think I can tell Dr. Baker.

(turns back to DR. BAKER)

We're trying to discover certain facts concerning the late Mrs. de Winter's activities on the day of her death, October the twelfth, last year. I want like you to tell me, if you can, whether any one of that name paid you a visit on that date.

DR. BAKER *(worried)*

I'm awfully sorry, but I'm afraid I can't help you. I should have remembered the name de Winter. I've never attended a Mrs. de Winter in my life.

FAVELL *(sharply)*

How could you possibly tell all your patients' names?

DR. BAKER

I can look it up in my engagement diary if you like.
(picks up engagement book from his desk)
Did you say the twelfth of October?

JULYAN

Yes.

DR. BAKER looks through his engagement book.

DR. BAKER

Ah, here we are . . . No . . . No de Winter.

FAVELL *(disappointed)*

Are you sure?

DR. BAKER

Here are all the appointments for that day . . . Ross . . . Campbell . . . Steadall . . . Perrino . . . Danvers . . . Matthews . . .

MAXIM *(suddenly cries out)*

Hold on!

FAVELL

Danny! What the devil . . .

Did you say Danvers?

DR. BAKER

Yes, I have Mrs. Danvers for three o'clock.

FAVELL

What did she look like? Can you remember?

DR. BAKER

Yes, I remember her quite well. She was a very beauti-ful woman—tall, dark, exquisitely dressed.

FRANK

Rebecca!

JULYAN

This lady must have used an assumed name.

DR. BAKER

Is that so? . . . This *is* a surprise! I'd known her for a long time.

FAVELL

What was the matter with her?

DR. BAKER *(interposes protestingly)*
My dear sir—there are certain ethics —

FRANK *(interrupting)*
Could you supply a reason, Dr. Baker, for Mrs. de Winter's suicide?

FAVELL (breaking in quickly)

For her *murder*, you mean! She was going to have a kid, wasn't she? Come on—out with it! Tell me, what else would a woman of her class be doing in a dump like this?

DR. BAKER

I assume that the official nature of this visit makes it necessary for me . . .

JULYAN

I assure you that we would not be troubling you if it were *not* necessary.

DR. BAKER

You want to know if I can suggest any motive as to why Mrs. de Winter should have taken her life? Yes, I think I can. The woman who called herself Mrs. Danvers was very seriously ill.

MAXIM

She was not going to have a child?

DR. BAKER

That was what she thought . . . But my diagnosis was different. I sent her to a well-known specialist for an examination and x-rays . . . and on this date, she returned to learn his report . . .

(he speaks gravely. All are listening intently.)

I remember her standing here holding out her hand for the photograph. "I want to know the truth," she said. "I don't want soft words and a bedside manner. If I'm for it, you can tell me right away." I knew that she was not the type to accept a lie. She asked for the truth, and I let her have it . . . She thanked me . . . I never saw her again, so I assumed . . .

MAXIM

What was wrong with her?

DR. BAKER

Cancer. Yes . . . The growth was deep-rooted. An operation would have been no earthly use at all. In a short time, she would have been under morphia. There was *nothing* that could be done for her—except wait.

MAXIM

Did she say anything—when you told her —

DR. BAKER

She smiled in a queer sort of way . . . Your wife was a wonderful woman, Mr. de Winter . . . and, oh yes . . . I remember she said something that struck me as being very peculiar at the time . . . When I told her it was a matter of months, she said, "Oh no, Doctor, not that long."

JULYAN

You've been very kind, and you have told us all we wanted to know. We shall probably need an official verification . . .

DR. BAKER

Verification?

JULYAN

Yes—to confirm the verdict of suicide.

DR. BAKER

I understand . . . Can I offer you gentlemen a glass of sherry?

JULYAN

No, very kind, but I think we ought to be going.

DISSOLVE TO:
EXT. DR. BAKER'S—NIGHT

The four come down from the doctor's house and over toward the cars at the curb.

FRANK

Thank Heaven we know the truth!

They have now all reached the cars at the curb.

JULYAN

Dreadful thing—dreadful. A young and lovely woman like that . . . No wonder.

FAVELL

I never had the remotest idea. Neither did Danny, I'm sure. Wish I had a drink!

FRANK

Will we be needed further at the inquest, Colonel Julyan?

JULYAN

No. I can see to it that Max is not troubled any further.

FAVELL

Are you ready to start, Colonel?

JULYAN

No, thank you. I'm staying in town tonight. And let me tell you, Favell, blackmail is not much of a profession. We know how to deal with it in our part of the world. Strange as it may seem to you.

FAVELL

I'm sure that I don't know what you're talking about! But if you ever need a new car, Colonel, just let me know.

FAVELL goes off.

MAXIM

Impossible to thank you for your kindness to us through all this. You know how I feel without my saying it.

JULYAN

Not at all. Put the whole thing behind you. But let your wife know, or she'll be getting worried.

MAXIM

Yes, of course I'll phone straight her at once, and we'll get straight along to Manderley.

As MAXIM goes off, JULYAN turns to FRANK.

JULYAN

Goodbye, Crawley. Maxim's got a great friend.

As JULYAN goes off, MAXIM returns. FRANK helps him put on his topcoat.

MAXIM

Frank.

FRANK

Yes, Maxim?

MAXIM

There's something you don't know. I didn't kill her, Frank . . .

(Frank's face betrays relief)

But I know now that when she told me about the child, she *wanted* me to kill her . . . She lied on purpose . . . She foresaw the whole thing . . . That's why she stood there laughing when she . . .

FRANK

Don't think about it any more.

MAXIM

Thank you, Frank.

DISSOLVE TO:
INT. STREET PHONE BOOTH—NIGHT

FAVELL is at the phone. He hears a reply in the receiver and speaks into the mouthpiece:

FAVELL *(bitterly)*

Hello, Danny . . . I just wanted to tell you the news . . . Rebecca held out on both of us . . . She had *cancer*! . . . Yes—suicide . . . And now Max and that dear little bride of his will be about to stay on at Manderley and live happily ever after . . . Bye bye, Danny.

FAVELL comes from the phone booth and walks to his car at the curb, where a POLICEMAN is standing.

POLICEMAN

Is this your car, sir?

FAVELL

Yes.

POLICEMAN

Will you be going soon? This isn't a parking place, you know.

FAVELL

Oh, isn't it? Well, people are entitled to leave their cars outside if they want to. It's a pity some of you fellows haven't anything better to do!

EXT. COUNTRY ROAD—NIGHT—
SEMI CLOSE UP

MAXIM and FRANK are driving back to Manderley.

FRANK

When you phoned her, did she say she'd wait up?

MAXIM

Yes—I asked her to go to bed, but she wouldn't hear of it. I wish I could get more speed out of this thing!

FRANK

Is something troubling you, Maxim?

MAXIM

I can't get over the feeling that something's wrong.

EXT. MANLERLEY—
LONG SHOT—HIGHT

While heavy clouds pass over the roof of Manderley, we see a strange light passing through the upper windows. The whole of the place is in darkness otherwise.

INT. HALL

From the top of the stairs we see ahead of us a moving light, which traverses the paneled walls and staircase. We follow it down and down until it reaches the open library door. The light passes through into the library and eventually reveals "I" asleep in a chair. The light also includes JASPER, who raises his head. There are a few nearly dead embers in the fireplace, which do not add to the light in the room.

We see the back of MRS. DANVERS' head and shoulders. She is carrying a lighted candle. She looks down at the sleeping "I" and then turns round into the camera, a mysterious, cunning look on her face, which is lit from below by the candle she holds.

EXT. COUNTRY ROAD—
LONG SHOT—NIGHT

On the country road, suddenly MAXIM pulls the car up with a jerk.

MAXIM

Frank.

FRANK

What's the matter? . . . why did we stop?

MAXIM

What time is it?

• 171 •

FRANK

This clock's wrong. It must be three or four. Why?

MAXIM

That can't be the dawn breaking over there.

FRANK

It's in the winter you see the Northern Lights, isn't it?

MAXIM

That's not the Northern Lights . . . That's Manderley!

MAXIM starts the car off frantically in a burst of speed.

Finally they come to the lawn in front of Manderley. The whole place is in flames. Furniture has been piled high in front of the house, servants moving about in their night attire.

MAXIM and FRANK get out of the car.

MAXIM

Frith, Frith!

FRITH

I thought I saw her, sir.

MAXIM

Where?

"I" comes, led by JASPER on a leash.

"I" *(rushing toward him)*

Maxim! Maxim!

She flies into his arms. He holds her silently and tightly to him, her face pressed against his coat.

"I"

Maxim, Maxim! Thank God you've come back to me!

MAXIM

My darling! Are you all right?

They kiss.

"I"

Mrs. Danvers. She's gone mad. She told me she'd rather destroy Manderley than see us happy here.

A SERVANT

Look! The west wing!

We see flames flashing through a window, and MRS. DANVERS rushing about inside, surrounded by flames. A flaming roof comes down on her head. It is Rebecca's room, and we see her bed and sheets, with the initial "R," also in flames.

THE END

ABOUT THE FILM

The 1940 film *Rebecca* is acclaimed as one of the greatest achievements of the legendary director Alfred Hitchcock.

Based on Daphne du Maurier's classic novel of the same name, it tells the story of an unnamed young woman who is trapped in a degrading job as a companion to a snobbish lady. She is rescued by the handsome, elegant, but enigmatic English gentleman Maxim de Winter, who marries her in a whirlwind romance and takes her to Manderley, his magnificent estate in Cornwall.

At Manderley, the heroine is confronted by a huge number of challenges: the dour and menacing Mrs. Danvers, who runs the household; servants the heroine does not know how to manage; and friends and relations of her husband's who derive a cruel amusement from her discomfort.

Most dismaying of all is Maxim's mysterious attitude toward his late wife, Rebecca, whose presence is still all over the house in the form of countless monograms. Even Rebecca's dog, Jasper, seems to spurn his new mistress. The heroine is constantly reminded of her husband's adoration of Rebecca and his inconsolable grief over her death at sea the previous year.

The truth about these matters is revealed step by step through Hitchcock's masterful hand. As usual, he merges plot, setting, and character to create a haunting and unforgettable picture of the cruelties of individuals—and of the English class system.

Rebecca is not a horror film in a conventional sense: there are no monsters, no supernatural elements. Yet in its way, the film is even more chilling in that it reveals the ultimate horror: the predilection for evil and self-deception in the human character.

The film is not all darkness. It constantly counterposes evil and malice with essential human decency, which is somehow able to stand up to—and triumph over—the bad side of human nature and reveal the promise of genuine love.

Rebecca is a masterpiece of cinema that speaks to the fears and hopes that live in all of us. It is an unforgettable experience that will change your life.